D1525624

ADVANCE PRAISE FOR

The Call of the VOID

"*The Call of the Void* offers a disturbing and unsettling worldview, a reality infused with creeping chaos and intricately laced with dark epiphanies that linger long after you close the covers."
—F. Paul Wilson

"Two unique literary voices have created a dark, disturbing tale."
—David Morrell

"Disturbing, dark, and shocking, this beautifully written novella asks questions with no easy answers, and it will echo with you long after the final page."
—Tim Lebbon

"*The Call of the Void* is like *Of Mice and Men* in that it is a packed short novel. It's a meditation on Time and our endless loops of ghost memories, recollections, imaginings, and possibilities. It's fictional, it's philosophical, and it treats the ways of the Cosmos and Humankind and the soul you see in your mirror."
—Mort Castle

The Call of the VOID

The Call of the Void

MICHAEL BAILEY

ERINN L. KEMPER

BLEEDING
EDGE BOOKS

THE CALL OF THE VOID
Copyright © 2022 by Michael Bailey & Erinn L. Kemper
All Rights Reserved

ISBN: 979-8432781543
Front cover & title design by Lynne Hansen | LynneHansenArt.com
Book design & formatting by Todd Keisling | Dullington Design Co.

This is a work of fiction. Names, characters, businesses, places, events, and incidents are either the products of the authors' imaginations or used in a fictitious manner. Any resemblance to actual persons, living or dead, or actual events is purely coincidental.

No part of this publication may be reproduced, stored in a retrieval system, or transmitted in any form or by any means, without the prior permission in writing of the publisher, nor be otherwise circulated in any form of binding or cover than that in which it is published and without a similar condition including this condition being imposed on the subsequent purchaser.

Bleeding Edge Books
www.bleedingedgepub.com

The Call of the VOID

1

L'appel Du Vide

he needed to be wanted. Kovelant flipped through his case notes. He circled the phrase and wrote a question mark next to it. 'Needed to be wanted,' not 'wanted to be needed.' Somehow Chloe Bisset had *needed* to weave into oncoming traffic that night, body thrown first through her own windshield and then through the windshield of the vehicle she'd struck, thus into the driver *her body* had struck, killing both women instantly. They had embraced before catching fire: a collection of crushed skull, interlace of ribcage, four arms and four legs.

On the morgue's examination table, under the glare of bright fluorescents, the women resembled a charred arachnid skeleton: two people, yet one—half the size of a normal body because of their destruction.

Kovelant had seen dead bodies over the years, but nothing like this.

MICHAEL BAILEY & ERINN L. KEMPER

Accident, he told himself, *this was no accident*.

He covered his mouth with a gloved hand as the coroner peeled one arm from another. What was left of the two women entwined, but the coroner—*Carl Hogan. His name's Carl. Your friend, not a job title*—was careful with the blade to separate where the women had cauterized together. His voice droned steadily over char breaking away from char as he recorded his findings.

"How can you tell one from the other?" Kovelant asked.

"At this point," Carl said, face shield reflecting the overhead lights, "only by bones; everything else..." he left it hanging, like the dangling arm he held, which had pulled free unexpectedly. "Humerus," he added, and then, "Too soon for jokes?"

Kovelant leaned against the wall, flipping to the first page of case notes he'd taken. His observations from the wreck pulled him back to the scene.

Other drivers, who pulled over after the accident or witnessed it happen firsthand, were out of their vehicles when Kovelant arrived with his lights blasting the dark. Many pointed at the ruin, some talking with their hands, some on phones, some recording video or snapping pictures for who-knows-what. Before he could get close enough to spot any casualties, the two vehicles that had become one in their violent dance ignited, a thing that rarely happened outside the world of cinema. He shielded his face with his hands, the heat of the vehicles' combined breath searing his eyes. Suddenly his job was to establish a perimeter because those around wanted to be close. *Everyone back! Just stay back!* He could do nothing but watch it all burn, the fire too hot, the risk of explosion too high...

"I heard she has a daughter," Carl said, bringing him back into the room, to the smell of burnt flesh. He was trying to strike up conversation, rekindle a friendship that had drifted over the years. But how many years had they lost of that past?

Had a daughter, Kovelant thought, but no, that wasn't right. She still *has* a daughter, this dead woman; it's the daughter who no longer has a mother. The daughter *had* a mother, he assured himself, *and we live inside our parents forever*, came the next thought, *and parents inside their children forever*, but one taken from the other fucked with the tense of 'to have.'

"We're supposed to go first," he said, and had to turn away, "the parents; not the other way around, but that doesn't make any of this right. No one should die in such a way."

They shared silence much like they had over the years. Kovelant could almost smell the whiskey fumes that accompanied those silences. Smokey like the artifacts on Carl's table.

"Strange to think Benz or Ford," Carl said, "or whoever takes credit for the automobile, maybe Studebaker, I don't know, would become the worst mass murderers of our time. I mean, they didn't dream of any of this shit happening, people dying by their inventions, but they've taken more than anyone. A morbid thought, even for someone in my profession, but—" Carl cleared his throat and coughed out what sounded like a suppressed gag, then set something down on the stainless-steel tray at his side. "Tesla, Edison... anyone, really, who introduces something new into the world. How many cellphones have distracted drivers into—" and again he caught himself. "Shit. Sorry."

"That's okay. Can't expect you to always have your filter on."

Kovelant turned back to the mess of bodies, limbs curled around one another. Something like this requires others to study what remained, to figure out what happened. Both women deserved an explanation; the families they left behind deserved an explanation. He walked around the table, took it all in, eyes watering for more than one reason.

Luckily no other vehicles were involved, and after the bulk of the accident had been cleared, he'd worked with a crash scene investigator who pointed out the twinned and barely perceptible rubber marks on the road, the reason for his further investigation.

Semicolon-like marks had fused to the road by the heat of the fire. Not from Bisset's sudden braking, but from what looked like a last-second shift across the asphalt before the impact. As if this woman, this Chloe Bisset, had pulled hard on her steering wheel to cross the double-yellows to hit the other vehicle. Not involuntary manslaughter / accidental death, but murder / suicide, to an extent. She'd *weaved*, and that baffled him.

Even the two vehicles had become one when her Ford Explorer and Montgomery's Volkswagen Whatever-It-Was—still undetermined—had collided head-on. He couldn't get the image out of his head: two back-ends of similarly shaped vehicles suddenly connected, their front-ends gone, and the people inside...

"Remember when Molly and Lili used to..." Carl said, and left that, too, hanging, catching himself, or throwing it out there on purpose.

Their kids used to play together, but no longer. Twenty-plus years, now. He pictured their three-year-olds giggling and running hand-in-hand over the park grass and *don't go too far, girls* one of their mothers would say, and the girls'd turn around and melt everyone with their smiles.

He wanted to talk, but couldn't, not over the dead.

"Let me know if you find anything," Kovelant said instead, shaken from the memory, but what exactly might be found in something as ugly as this?

There was nothing but that itching to determine *why* the woman had swerved across lanes last-second, *why* she had chosen to end both her life and in turn this other woman's. Something had called him to the dual-autopsy, for closure he knew deep down would never come, at least not from this. He needed to see Chloe Bisset one last time to let the reality of the situation sink in, or he needed someone to talk to, needed Carl's voice, his ears...

A clink of metal on metal as the coroner dropped a round metal object onto the stainless tray, *spinning, spinning, spinning*, in anticipation, much like a spun coin, then settling.

EVIDENCE

Agency: <u>Sacramento County Coroner's Office</u>
Collected by: <u>Carl Hogan</u>
Item #: <u>0005</u>   Case #: <u>2019-08249273</u>
Date: <u>04/16/19</u>   Time: <u>15:24</u>
Description: <u>Silver ring</u>

Location: <u>Worn on the deceased, Chloe Bisset,</u>
          <u>ring finger (L)</u>
Remarks: <u>Smooth and slightly convex exterior,</u>
         <u>underside engraving (name illegible)</u>

Driving home, Kovelant's thoughts wandered to the road, to those yellow parallel lines separating one side of the freeway from the next. How easy it would be to simply yank the wheel, to cross over ten or so feet of traffic and plow into an oncoming vehicle. The speed limit was posted as sixty-five, but everyone, even he, drove seventy-five, on average. Too many vehicles speeding for the California Highway Patrol to monitor and enforce properly.

How easy it would be.

"Playing Pac-Man," he used to call it, veering over the divide by accident, the little round light-reflective warning bumps *bump-bump-bumping* under tires. His head was spinning, spinning, spinning, and wouldn't settle. "Driving by Braille," his father used to say.

And had Kovelant himself not had his own urges on rare occasion, to cross the parallel yellows and hit another car, to veer into a streetlight, a mailbox, a brick wall? Had he not walked the edge of life's razor now and again: peering over the side of a cliff, wondering what it would be like to free-fall, what it would be like to pull the handle of a plane's emergency door while in flight, or tempting death in other ways?

Some preferred to sky-dive, ride rollercoasters, rock-climb, race vehicles, parkour over rooftops, but why the desire for adrenaline? What was his rush?

When you have self-destructive thoughts, even for a split second, what did that mean, even if you'd never follow through?

How easy it would be...

L'appel du vide, he discovered in his research, was both an explanation and a non-explanation for what had happened. The phrase translated to "the call of the void," which didn't surprise him, for the French often had ways of expressing the otherwise unexplainable: *déjà vu* for "already seen," *jamais vu*, for its polar opposite, even *je dis ça, je dis rien*, which didn't mean anything at all, other than "just saying." As useless as the word 'actually.'

The "vertigo of possibility" it was sometimes called, this feeling of *l'appel du vide:* a means of contemplating experiments in freedom otherwise never considered.

But in the case of Chloe Bisset—a French name, no less—there had to be something more. There had to be a meaning to her madness, a reason for taking not only *her* life, but this other woman's. Most would never answer the call of the void, but only briefly contemplate what *could* happen. No, Bisset had also taken Sue Montgomery's life in her last-second decision, thus changing the course of futures for two families and everyone in them—a foul weave of death.

The voice of three-year-old Maxie, asking *where's mommy?* echoed in his mind. He imagined Chloe's husband, Jules, having to explain *there was an accident, your mommy's in heaven now*. He imagined what Sue Montgomery must have seen in that split-second before her life ended: headlights fluttering in front of her, a flicker, really, no time to brake or swerve like the suddenly-there vehicle. The last thing she ever saw: Chloe Bisset's eyes. Not only had the vehicles hit head-on, but—

His phone vibrated. "Kovelant," he said, pressing the phone to his ear to help him focus. Somehow, he knew it would be the coroner. *Déjà vu.*

"Hey, John. It's Carl."

He must've found something small, something insignificant to *him* but significant to the case, and he'd phrase it that way, this little something he'd found.

"What did you find?"

"Nothing big, but you know how these things go—a hair, a fiber, something foreign in the stomach, such trivial things sometimes have meaning, and can lead to bigger things, but—"

"What did you find?" Kovelant asked again, as if forcing the "already seen" to reveal itself and be seen again without all the unnecessary confusion and small talk.

"That ring, the wedding band on your *mademoiselle* Bisset."

"*Madame.* She was married," he said. "We know this already."

"She was, yes, but happily?"

"What does that have to do with anything?"

"Like I said, sometimes trivial things have meaning, not to *me*, but can lead to bigger things, to people like *you*, the all-powerful 'askers of important of questions.' So, I guess what I'm saying is this is where you ask the next important question."

A wedding ring, so what? She was married, and quite happily, according to her husband, and according to a girl friend at work. Little things, leading to bigger things, always something small, insignificant to all but few...

"There's something strange about the ring," Kovelant said.

"Not quite a question, but I'll answer it anyway with a '*Sí, mi amigo*,' or should I say '*Oui, mon ami*,' which is *friend*, not *lover*, right? I always get those two mixed up. Either way, yes, something strange with the ring."

"An inscription?" Kovelant said, the answer—another

question, in a way—coming to him instantly. It was either that, or a fake gem. "What does it say?"

"*Free. Together. Forever, Kristoph*, it reads, with a comma before and after the name, a nice little scripty-font, or it's *Kristopher* because the letters are a little smudged at the end. Hard to read, fire taking its toll and all. Didn't you say the husband's name was Jules?"

"Not the other woman's finger, I take it, not Montgomery's?" he said, but he knew the answer already. Ms. Montgomery wasn't married. She was a student, twenty-something years old, had a roommate until recently. He hadn't spoken to many people from her side of the story yet.

"Nope. Certain beyond a doubt," Carl said. "Dental records belonging to the bones of the body once wearing the ring link to that of *madame* Bisset."

"Could be a nickname for her husband, or maybe his middle name," he said, thinking aloud, but that wasn't right, either. Her husband's middle name started with an A. Adrian or Alexander or something. He had the file in front of him so he flipped through his overly detailed notes. "Tag it and bag it. I'll be right there," he said, hanging up.

Kovelant imagined his friend on the other end, feeling discarded, saying something like, "Nice talking to you as well, *mi amigo*" before getting back to his work.

And then he found it: Chloe Bisset's husband's full name, written clearly in his ugly pen-and-paper notetaking: Jules Alexander Bisset.

The final *comma* in the inscription bugged him. Similar in shape to the rubber marks on the road from the tires suddenly veering, like there was something more after this smallest of characters. With the comma, the inscription circled round and round, never ending. The situation gave it an ominous tone. *Forever, Kristoph,* and *Kristoph, Forever,* as in *I'm never gone, Kristoph, you can't get rid of me. Toujours proche.*

2

Hypothesis: If... then...

Chloe tucked her hand, the one with the wedding ring, under her purse when the man sat next to her on the bus. A perfect test subject: a few years younger than her, nice suit, scruffy hair, neck a little too long. Two weeks into the experiment and the results were mixed. The jelly Maxie had dripped on her skirt still felt sticky despite a quick cleaning. One of the joys of motherhood.

She curled her fingers into a fist.

Out the window, gardens and sun-crisped lawns faded into a blur as her attention shifted to the man. His leg. Her leg.

Ever so slowly, Chloe let the weight of her leg fall in his direction. With each bob and sway, as the bus rolled its cargo, she let the pressure increase, eased against him.

Older men tended to adjust their position, sever contact. Younger men, earbuds pinned to their ears, took no notice. This guy, mid-thirties—nice suit, strappy leather satchel perched on his lap—didn't react at first. The heat of him seeped through his pant-leg and her nylon stockings. And he pressed back in increments until their contact was no longer incidental.

When the bus rounded a corner and the man slid even closer, so now not just their knees but thighs and hips pressed close, Chloe focused on his reflection in the window. He sat with his head bowed, eyes closed. Was his expression neutral or did a smile flit across his lips?

Chloe pulled the stop-request wire.

"Sorry, excuse me." She shifted, breaking contact. "My stop."

He smiled. Just a regular smile, nothing suggestive. He got up and moved into the aisle, gripping an overhead bar to steady himself as the bus lurched to a stop.

Chloe ducked under his arm and hustled off the bus, the doors hissing shut behind her only a few blocks from her regular coffee shop.

She pondered the new data. The man had pressed back. She could still feel the presence of his leg, a warm tingle down her thigh. That and the fact that she'd worn her new pale-pink pumps, her 'triple-p's' as Jules called them, adding an extra wiggle to her step.

Her mind drifted as she joined the lemmings in the coffee line. When she got near the front, her hopes that today would be different deflated.

"You can pick up your coffee at the end of the counter. Have a wonderful day." The barista, Nikki according to her name tag—though yesterday it had been Ruth, and before that Sam—turned to take Chloe's order and her smile faded. "What'll you have?"

'Nikki', white-blonde hair pulled up into a sloppy bun, wore tight jeans and a baggy shirt with a pin that read 'NO NUKES' over her bony frame. Normally Wednesday was Nikki's day off.

"I'll have a quad-shot, half-sweet vanilla latte."

Same drink she'd ordered from Nikki for over a year.

"Sorry, what?" The barista looked out the window behind Chloe.

A man cleared his throat from further back in line. "You heard her. Go ahead and write up the order," he said.

Chloe glanced over her shoulder. The guy from the bus. A flush of heat rose from the collar of her button-down office shirt.

Nikki glared, her over-large eyes glinting, as she Sharpied "Clowy" on a cup.

Every damn time, and on purpose, the name was wrong.

"Hey, have you tried one of these?" The man reached around Chloe and pulled a card from a bowl in front of the till. A sign next to the bowl read CONUNDRUMS FOR THE CURIOUS. DON'T TAKE ONE. "This one says 'I have no hands, but knock on your door, sometimes quiet, sometimes loud. You rarely know when I pass you by, but if you catch me, you might fly.'"

Nikki sighed as she capped the marker.

Chloe scrunched her nose. *What knocks and passes by?* "I don't know. Maybe *opportunity?*"

He clapped his hands. "I think she's got it. What's the reward?"

"Lucky you." Nikki held out a hole punch. "You get credit toward a free drink of your choice. Where's your card?"

"I don't have one," she lied.

She had one in her purse, in fact, all the stories of the artsy building on the card were punched out, but how embarrassing would it be to use it now? She'd get a combo snort and eyeroll, or worse.

"*C'est dommage*," Nikki said, mocking Chloe's accent, and tipped an empty box on the counter. "We're clean out. I guess I'll just grant a wish." She smirked and looked over Chloe's shoulder. "Can I help the next person?"

Hot latte in hand, Chloe sat at her usual table and pulled out her phone. Sleepy-eyed office jockeys streamed in and texted while they waited to order. The windows streamed with a rippling haze of body heat.

"Mind if I join you? Name's Kris."

She tipped her cup, lava rolling down her fingers. Same guy.

"Oh, um..." She didn't know how to refuse without sounding rude, and then it was too late; he was already seated. "Chloe."

He pointed at the scribbled name on her cup, and then rotated his own so she could read his own barista-translated name—a K and a squiggly don't-give-two-shits wavy line.

"And check it out," he said, sliding a new Soul punch card across the table. "I asked man-bun working the espresso if they had any more. She was messing with you or didn't know. Something's off about that chick. You can use it next time."

"Thanks." She tucked the card in her pocket, then noticed she still had latte on her fingers and reached for a napkin.

"That barista is such an asshole." Kris gazed at the coffee counter, his expression turning thoughtful. "You know. In a way, I kinda admire the fact that she chooses to be an asshole. She's just doing her thing, and nobody really calls her on it. You can probably get away with a lot—people are so focused on themselves they rarely look up and see what's going on around them."

Chloe picked her purse up from the floor and picked up her phone. "Well, it was nice to meet you, K-squiggle, and thanks for the save, but I'd better get to—"

"No." Kris placed a hand on her forearm, pinning it to the table, urgency sharpening his voice. "Wait a sec."

"What?" She held on to her phone, willing to leave the latte if it meant getting away from this guy with the weird glint in his eyes. Heart quickening, she readied to flee.

"Hear me out. Forget work. Call in sick, or whatever. Ever do that? I think not. You're like me, sleepwalking your routine 'cause you got nothing better to do." His grin shed years from his face. "Just for once, say 'fuck it.' Do what you want, whatever that is." He knocked on the table. "Opportunity."

She shook her head, but excitement churned deep in her belly. She tried to suppress it, but whatever this guy had was contagious and she found herself leaning in.

"Just play hooky," she said, "simple as that?"

He pulled his phone from his pocket and dialed, eyes on her. Two rings, then two more, and yet another. A smile. "Hey, Jim. I'm not going to make it in today." A pause. "No, nothing like that. I need a 'me' day." He waited for a response and mouthed *need* to her, teeth all sparkly. After instructions for his colleagues, he said "*au revoir*" and winked.

He nudged her cellphone on the table.

"Your turn."

Chloe no longer needed caffeine. The shot of adrenaline from calling her boss with a concocted story about bad oysters had her keyed up, nerves jangling. Kris held out his elbow for her to take it as they left the café, but after a moment the triangle of elbow and arm fell flat as she took the lead, heading to the memorial park where she liked to lunch on cooler days.

She pointed to a bench in the shade.

"A good spot to brainstorm?"

"Nah. over here." Kris patted one of the gravestones, a rectangular box with a trumpeting angel perched on top. "Better for delinquents like us."

The granite still held the previous night's chill, and bore the name of two children, same birth and death day. Chloe shivered as she sat on the edge of the one belonging to the parents.

"Wherever our impulse takes us, that's where we go?"

"Just walk around and when something strikes us, *we* strike." He clapped his hands, sending pigeons flutter-scattering. "Like lightening. Then we move on."

Towering office buildings surrounded them. A massive

flock of starlings flitted along their alleys, gathering into a black ball, a 'murmuration' as Jules called them, then stretching into a long tube as they swooped around a church tower.

"Follow those birds," Kris said and threw his cup in a trash bin.

Chloe's bounced on the rim and toppled in. A sign.

Heart pounding, she raced after him. She pictured her new shoes striking sparks on the pavement. They ran past the church, along an alley, and eventually walked—panting and holding their sides when pain stitched their ribcages—across the Tower Bridge to a vacant construction site where the birds settled on a crane.

She surveyed the abandoned site. "It's like the carpenters all holstered their hammers and disappeared."

They used a scaffold as a jungle-gym, swinging hand-over-hand until losing grip, palms shiny with the promise of blisters. Chloe laughed so hard vanilla latte rose from her stomach in a sweet, creamy-bile gorge. She swallowed it back down.

Then the chase was on again as the birds rose in a dark cloud and devoured the sun, heading amoeba-like toward the state capitol building for a worm-feast at the park, or a breakfast burrito dropped by an office slouch trudging to his desk job.

"I'm a little hungry," Chloe said. "All I've had is a coffee." She gasped for air, hands on her knees, her feet feeling over-large in her new shoes, body reminding her that she no longer had the energy of her youth. "Wouldn't mind sitting for a minute, anyway."

Arm-in-arm, they skipped down Capitol Avenue, technically "M Street," although it wasn't called that since the street lettering went from L to N. They saluted any who glanced up from their devices. Chloe blew a kiss at a bearded old man in a Tilley hat, and he caught and put the phantom kiss in his pocket. "For later," he called out and attempted a wobbly skip of his own into a building when the doors sucked open to accept him.

Chloe scanned diners and street-side cafes for something that caught her fancy. At one of those brunch places where people line up down the block to eat fried chicken on waffles or pancakes seasoned with candied bacon, Kris pointed to a recently vacated table where two half-finished plates heaped with potatoes and toast spears had yet to attract flies.

"Breakfast is served." He stepped over the velvet rope and pulled out a chair.

Chloe blushed, angled away from the line of people waiting their turns, and hesitated.

"Pass the hot sauce," she said and swept a sprig of parsley off her chair. She'd burn away any germs.

Kris dug into his hijacked potatoes, smacking his lips and wiping a smear of hollandaise from Chloe's plate with a piece of toast.

"You gonna finish that?" he asked the woman at the next table over and grabbed her plate before she could toss a crumpled napkin on her half-eaten omelet. "No sense letting good food go to waste, right?"

Chloe grinned and took another bite. The potatoes were cold and no longer crispy, but they tasted great. She never ate at places like this, always reluctant to ask Jules to spend half a morning standing outside, Maxie restless with confusion as to why she had to wait to eat. The people in this line, the ones who weren't shooting her and Kris disgusted or angry looks, had to-go cups and expectant smiles. They chatted in clusters, and when the restaurant door opened, they peered down the line to see who was coming out. Each time the line shuffled forward, the people in front laughed louder, gestured more broadly.

Jules would hate these people. He liked his milky oatmeal sprinkled with raisins and brown sugar, every damn morning. Coffee and OJ. Routine, then off to work.

"Shit. We've been made." Kris scooped a final mouthful of omelet, threw a few dollars on the table, and hopped over the barricade, then crouched and cupped his hands like stirrups. "My lady, your chariot awaits."

Chloe dropped a dollar on top of his and stepped over the rope. She hitched her skirt up and jumped on his back, focusing on memories of her dad piggy-backing her home from the park, rather than the sensation of a strange man between her legs. She waved an invisible hat in the air with cowgirl flourish. Kris ran down the block with her jouncing up and down, her chin hitting his shoulder hard enough to rattle her teeth. He turned up an alley full of cardboard homes—their owners off scavenging—then set her down.

"You look a lot lighter than you are." He huffed and pressed a hand into his side. "Probably shouldn't have quit going to the gym."

"You're in all right shape." Chloe smoothed down her

skirt. "What next? I've always wanted to jump on the back of a garbage truck."

"I've always wanted to stick my head down a manhole and yell 'look out below.'"

"What if the person down there gets electrocuted or something."

"The cost of living, right? Expect the unexpected."

He was still bent over, not recovered.

Chloe took advantage and smacked him on the arm. "Tag, you're it."

Despite the lump of potatoes and hot sauce in her gut, she ran back out to the street, weaving through a swarm of people boarding and getting off a bus. Kris chased after her, cutting the distance rapidly. He wasn't hobbled by fancy new high-heeled shoes.

She took cover behind a cluster of students on a smoke break and called out, "You'll never catch me," and giggled, as the expression on the student in front of her changed from concerned to puzzled.

Kris caught up and tapped the student on his shoulder. "You're it."

After lunch at the local soup kitchen—ignoring dirty looks from volunteers and accepting a seat next to a giant of a man popping out of medium-sized clothes—they played "Checked by Texter." Spotting distracted text-walkers, they'd adjust their trajectory for collision.

"Watch where you're going," Chloe shouted angrily in each face as they collided, waiting until they scuttled off before sharing a laugh with Kris.

"I've gotta pee," she said, and leaned against the brick wall of the courthouse. "You see a bathroom?"

"There's one in the courthouse. You could share butt germs with a felon. Maybe a murderer if you're lucky."

A garbage truck beeped backward out of an alley on the other side of the street, and she would have chased after it and hitched a ride for a block or so if nature weren't pressing so hard.

"Be right back."

Chloe hobbled to the other side of the now-empty dumpster and squatted. She listened for footsteps, the ache growing, and was not able to relax enough. This was easier for guys. A sticker for a punk show at a local bar caught her eye, and her bladder let loose.

She swallowed against a wave of sadness. She used to go to shows with Jules, all the time. That was their thing. They were the cool married couple who moshed, went on last-minute road trips, ate sushi in bed at 2:00 A.M. after a bottle of wine on the beach at sunset, often followed by lovemaking under the stars, which one time led to a surprise she'd never been ready for: Maxie.

As she pissed, she thought how pissed Jules would be, or disappointed at least, if she weren't home to feed, bathe, and tuck in their daughter. Routine.

She tugged at her skirt as she emerged from the alley.

Kris stood on the plinth of a lamppost, holding on

31

one-armed. Behind him, next to the golden Tower Bridge, a crumbling old building beckoned her with its plywood-covered windows. Some of the exposed windows were blown out completely, staring upon them like empty black sockets, inviting her inside.

"I know what I want to do," she said.

3
Je ne sais pas

hy had she weaved into traffic? Kovelant wondered again. *It just didn't make sense.*

None of it made sense: the ring, the two entangled bodies, Chloe Bisset's story—at least as told by those who knew her or were around her daily. Her husband was a mess, and so was little Maxie. Everyone he'd interviewed had shown nothing but surprise, with not even a hint of "Yeah, she was suicidal" or "I could see her doing such a thing." No, none of it made a lick of sense, and so he moved on to the other woman: Sue Montgomery.

She was single, *happily* single. She lived in an apartment downtown, an older building, but with charm, and dishes laid out for a cat. Part-time barista, part-time student at the university. Her bedside table stacked with half-read textbooks: Norton's Anthologies, translations of Herodotus and Homer. No Kristophs in her side of the story. She had been driving out to meet up with someone at a bar called The Stagger Inn—according to a note on her fridge—and her life had suddenly ended in the spark of time it took for the two vehicles to smash into each other. There was nothing linking the two women, other than their entangled bodies.

Kovelant thought of the coroner prying the two women apart, thought of the selfies of Sue Montgomery and her friends he'd seen in picture frames bringing life to her otherwise dead apartment, as well as those stuck to the refrigerator. There were magnetic letters on the door, like those you'd have for a kid to practice spelling instead of raiding the fridge, and some had been arranged into GOT SEX? and others into MILK and CHEESE and perhaps a few other things this woman and her roommate needed. There were phone numbers on the fridge as well, scribbled on Post-It notes of various color, all of which he had jotted down in his notetaking. One number led him to Luigi's Pizza, and another to Soul, the coffee shop where she'd worked. A third rang busy and always went to a not-yet-setup voicemail box. He'd called the number, left his name and title and contact info, but so far no one had called him back.

As far as he could tell, all Sue's friends were women. She may have been into women herself, not that any of that mattered, other than distancing her own story from that of this Kristoph fellow.

Maybe that was the connection with Chloe Bisset? *This is* her *story,* he mused.

Sue's roommate had recently moved out. Kovelant sensed tension there, though the woman was clearly shaken by the news. The name 'Chloe' didn't ring a bell, nor 'Kristoph,' and the young woman tilted her head and touched her badly dyed, pink-red-blond hair self-consciously. Contemplating, not lying. He'd taken courses on tics people offer when hiding truths. She'd spoken earnestly, *wanting* to help.

News of death spreads virally, to family, neighbors, colleagues, other parents at playdates. *Did you hear and did you hear and did you hear.* Those not in the mix got their information just as quickly from the news or from the paper or during watercooler talk. "Did you hear about Sue Montgomery / Chloe Bisset? So tragic."

But when is death not tragic?

CHAIN OF CUSTODY

Received from: Carl Hogan, Coroner

By: Ben Tamsen, Forensics Tech.,
Sacramento CSI Unit

Date: 04/16/19   **Time:** 15:18

CHAIN OF CUSTODY

Received from: Ben Tamsen, FT

By: John Kovelant, Det. Sgt, Sac County
Sheriff's Dept.

Date: 04/16/19   **Time:** 17:30

The ring was as ordinary as the coroner had described: smooth silver—*possibly* silver, but most likely an alloy containing silver—with the inscription and the name, Kristoph, not Kristopher, for forensics had finished cleaning the ring and there were no more letters.

EVIDENCE

Agency: <u>Sacramento County Sheriff's Department</u>

Collected by: <u>John Kovelant</u>

Item #: <u>0013</u>   **Case #:** <u>2019-08249273</u>

Date: <u>04/15/19</u>   **Time:** <u>03:24</u>

Description: <u>Receipt (partial)</u>

Location: <u>Stuck to chain-link fence next to the accident, along with other paper debris (see items 0014 – 0028)</u>

Remarks: <u>Purchase from The Stagger Inn, time-stamped 11:51 p.m., amount section missing, burned edges</u>

Kovelant didn't need to cut the red sealing tape, but kept the evidence bag long enough to take his own digital pictures, through the plastic. There were other evidence bags from the "crime scene"—as it was being called unless he proved otherwise—and most of it collected by him and his team once cleared to do so. Everything sealed, catalogued.

The receipt put Bisset at the bar before midnight, a window of less than an hour between closing her tab and the unfortunate 'accident,' given it had taken him the rest of the gap in time to make it to the scene.

Why was she there, so late, without her husband?

Bisset had been leaving the bar, Montgomery going there. Two ships colliding in the night.

How he had even found the receipt, partially intact, was a bit of luck. Kovelant figured she'd slipped it in her purse and not her pocket before leaving the bar. They'd found the purse tossed, like her, through the window, then somehow it had tumbled down the street *next* to the burning vehicles, not *within* them. Other articles from her purse had littered the scene: a tube of lipstick, feminine products, coins, a compact mirror, a wallet, a five and two ones, a small plastic rose, a kids' puzzle book, other receipts, other 'evidence.'

Was Jules at home, reading in bed, pondering Chloe's whereabouts, with Maxie sound asleep? "We tried texting her," he'd said, and then hours later... dead.

Kovelant and his team had found these items on the street, then, the papers blown around, and he sorted through them again: Item #0029, a small can of pepper spray; Item #0047, a pen from her work, address etched onto the side; Item #0040, a credit / debit card; Item #0041, a punch-card for some coffee shop in mid-town. Item #0039, half a tube of Mentos. It wasn't until he was about to give up looking, having lifted Item #0015 from the box, when he found something that tickled the curious itch in his mind, something he'd found clinging to a stretch of fence. He'd collected it himself although couldn't remember—

EVIDENCE

Agency: <u>Sacramento County Sheriff's Department</u>

Collected by: <u>John Kovelant</u>

Item #: <u>0015</u>   Case #: <u>2019-08249273</u>

Date: <u>04/15/19</u> Time: <u>03:41</u>

Description: <u>Post-It note (blue)</u>

Location: <u>Stuck to chain-link fence next to the accident, along with other paper debris (see items 0014 – 0028)</u>

Remarks: <u>Handwritten note (from Chloe? check hand-writing samples for comparison)</u>

The blue note contained a phone number in a loopy script, feminine. Chloe's handwriting, most likely. He'd forgotten about it until now, which he guessed was the point of cataloguing evidence, so things *couldn't* be forgotten.

Kovelant called the number and let it ring until he put it together that it must be a land line. Could be someone's home number, he realized, or a business with no one left around to answer. No automated voice. Eleven rings before he ended the call. It was close to 18:00, so the number might belong to a now-closed business—the bar—or someone more old-school, someone not at home.

When's the last time anyone used an answering machine?

Cellular had taken over for as long back as he cared to remember. Land lines all but extinct. Voicemail replacing answering machines. Wireless replacing cords. Pagers, calculators, notepads, alarms, fax machines, cameras, maps / GPS; all had been replaced by phones in one way or another, their owners lost without them. They hadn't found a cell phone in the carnage, which was the first thing he looked for, in most cases. He'd sent many damaged cell phones over the years to CSI to retrieve information; usually they could get stuff off them using their magic. Cell phones were perhaps *the* most important of items one could find at a crime scene.

If *this is a crime scene,* he pondered, *this crash, this 'accident.'*

Chloe Bisset's phone was melted, part of the car now, part of the dashboard, melted into *her.* He imagined the thing propped in a cup holder while charging or stuck against one of the vents with some grippy thing so she could have it close while driving. Now, it was gone, along with the important stuff it once contained.

The handwriting on the note, though, he was sure it belonged to Chloe Bisset. The multi-car fire hadn't taken that away from her, even after death. The note was one of the few physical things she'd left behind, like the ring, as ghostly as the air in a balloon found post-party from someone who'd died. A part of him knew Mr. Bisset would want the note—

Jules, her husband; he has a name. His wife was gone; he'd want whatever he could get.

Who'd get the ring? he wondered.

There was a checkbook with the rest of the evidence, Kovelant remembered, something he could use for comparison. Numbers, and lots of them. She was old-school, still used paper money and check registers. He had catalogued a checkbook, and yes, there it was with the rest of the items found by the chain-link fence, Item #0028. He flipped through the register, compared swirly sixes and nines, loops of zeros and eights, dashes through the sevens, little hooks on the tips of each one and slants on the tops of threes and fives. The numbers in the register matched those on the blue Post-It note—an address for The Stagger Inn.

He guessed it made sense she'd have written it down. This meant she'd made an appointment at the bar. Or a date with this Kristoph fellow. He knew the bar, had a whiskey now and again while off-duty, and he'd been called there on occasion to handle a few drunkards trying to drive their way home.

"Forensics found her ring," he said into his phone, and there was silence for a while from Jules Bisset on the other end. "I'd like to meet you somewhere to talk about it. Maybe over coffee?"

Jules let out a shuddering breath. "I'll get that back, right? Is it—"

"We'll have it cleaned for you."

Another long silence.

"Once we're done with it, it's yours," Kovelant told him. "Following procedure, is all, everything shot and documented. We can talk about next steps. Your place okay? I'd like to ask you some questions to clarify a few things. Won't take much of your time, nothing formal. I know you've been through a lot these last few days and the station's not somewhere you want to be again so soon, so let's meet at your place... let's say noon."

The station would be more proper, but subtly insisting the meeting be at the Bisset residence would offer things he couldn't get at the station. Jules refusing to meet at home would imply something hidden there, something Kovelant wasn't supposed to see. Pictures on the walls, knickknacks on the shelves, little freely-offered insights into their everyday lives. Something missing from the case notes, not collected in evidence bags. Kovelant had chosen the time to meet because noon was only thirty minutes away, and it would take him at least twenty to get there. Time against him. Time able to hide things. Time sometimes moving too fast.

A hesitation, and then, "Maxie's having a play date at her grandma's to keep her mind occupied, so noon would be fine. I could put on a fresh pot. Going through coffee like water."

Jules Bisset didn't seem like the type who'd have anything to hide, or would do so willingly, but there was something about the hesitation that concerned him; as if Mr. Bisset had something to say, but didn't quite know how to say it, or if he *should*.

Kovelant knew what he wanted to ask, and could have done so over the phone, but person-to-person was better. Eyes had difficulty hiding lies, and likewise told hidden truths.

On the drive there, he called the number on the Post-It again. After ringing a half-dozen times, a woman answered, which surprised him. He'd expected the rings to last forever, looked down at his wedding band. *Doesn't everyone…*

"'Stagger Inn," she said, as if it were an invitation.

And eventually stagger out, Kovelant thought.

"Hello?" the woman said.

"Sorry, this is Detective Kovelant of the Sacramento County Sheriff's Office. This number came up in my case notes. I'm just calling to verify the number."

"The French woman, right? From the accident a few nights ago?"

He was shocked at first, hearing the barkeep's familiarity with the case, but the story had spread, and this woman, if she'd been working that night, would have recognized the picture of Chloe Bisset making the rounds in papers and newscasts: a shot of her smiling, slightly turned away from the camera—*camera phone*, he assumed—toward the ocean. Kovelant had recognized the picture as that of her profile image from social media.

"That's correct," he said.

"She was here that night, just before—" she started, and then interrupted herself. "She left here sober, only drank 'vodka tonic, sans the vodka,' at least that's how she ordered them. She had two or three," she offered, "nothing with alcohol."

Pregnant? he jotted in his notebook.

"Was she with anyone?"

"Hit on plenty, but alone. Left by herself."

"Do you remember if she was waiting for someone?"

"She checked her phone a lot, so does everyone, right?"

He asked a few more questions, but the night had been busy, like most nights.

4

Prediction: Controls and Variables

At first Chloe didn't recognize Kris standing at the bus stop a few doors down from their coffee shop in his hoodie and jeans. He looked younger and smaller. She'd put on yoga pants and a tunic top, but that was classic soccer mom garb, so she swapped the yoga pants for the stretchy black jeans she used to go clubbing in back in her Uni days. They both had backpacks slung over their shoulders. Essentials for a night of prowling. Chloe's contained bottles of water, two flashlights—she wasn't going to be a horror movie cliché dropping her only light source and then fumbling around in the dark while danger inched ever closer—and granola bars, stuff she'd pack for a day out with Maxie.

"You ready to slay dragons?" she said.

Kris's eyes glittered, showing too much white in the streetlight, and he shadow-boxed an imagined foe. "They don't stand a chance." His voice sounded different, pitched like he might burst into manic laughter.

He wore a wedding ring, almost identical to the ring she'd gotten for Jules; a simple band, perhaps even the same. Had he worn it before? She instinctively reached for her own plain band, to hide it, but spun it around instead, as though calling Kris's attention to it. He seemed not to notice or tried to appear not to notice.

"How long have you—?" she said but was cut short.

The lights inside Soul winked out, and the door opened. 'Nikki' peered up and down the street, then turned and locked the door.

Chloe stepped closer to the buildings, not wanting to be recognized. "What the hell is she doing still working?" What she'd wanted to ask was how long he'd been married. She knew the conversation would eventually come up. How long could they pretend they each weren't concerned about running around together like this, or being caught?

"Split shift?" Kris said and shrugged. "It's a bit early for our B and E. Should we see where your favorite barista resides?"

"Let's tail." Chloe rubbed her hands together, trying to picture the burrow 'Nikki' called home. A basement under her parents' house? A loft with a menagerie of cats howling for dinner? One of those share houses with Bob Marley banners for curtains?

Nikki pulled her phone out of her jacket pocket and answered. She faced the window of the bookshop and pushed her hair back from her eyes, then pulled it forward again. "Yeah. I'm coming. I just gotta grab my things."

Chloe adjusted her pack, ready to follow, but Nikki

stopped three doors down from the coffee shop and pushed open a steel door.

"Well, that was quick." Kris sounded disappointed, but his lips curled in a grin as he moved across the sidewalk and looked up at the building. Chloe joined him. "Second floor, middle, a light just went on."

"Home sweet home," Chloe said. "Let's hang for a bit, since it sounded like she was heading right back out. She's going to meet her boyfriend, or girlfriend, or, I don't know, she's polyamorous. Someone in a band with a neck tattoo."

Kris tucked his hands into his pockets and leaned against the wall. "So, you do anything after we parted ways?" The way he said 'anything' made it clear he meant 'anything unusual.'

Chloe considered telling him how the house had been empty when she got home and, as usual, she'd caught her purse strap on Jules's golf bag, sending it clattering to the floor. He kept it by the door, ready for when he needed 'down time' which always seemed to coincide with days when she and Maxie had a few free hours. It only took two good swings to open a big enough hole in the drywall to drop the golf club in, then she'd rehung their most recent family portrait. But she didn't want to bring up Jules and Maxie. Not now. Not ever.

"Well, I had breakfast for dinner," she said, "and ate in front of the TV."

"You badass."

"How about you?"

Kris's breath caught, and he shoved his hands deeper in his pockets. "Yeah, nothing much. Just got ready for tonight."

Nothing much?

The door to Nikki's building swung open.

"Here we go." Chloe braced, ready to follow, but Nikki, in a fresh shirt with a bulging overnight bag, clicked a key fob and a car blipped in reply, an SUV parked behind them with a pink plastic unicorn glued on as a hood ornament, posed ready to charge. There was nowhere to hide, and the barista would have to walk past them unless they hurried off in the other direction, which would draw her attention, too.

"Oh shit," Chloe said, mostly as an exhale.

"I got an idea," Kris said and pushed her back against the brick wall, roughly but not, although her skull connected and created stars. He wrapped himself around her, one hand behind her head, the other behind the small of her back.

"I'm pretty sure I saw this in a movie," Chloe whispered.

Kris chuckled softly and pressed her head to his neck as he buried his face into her collar bone. Just two high schoolers unashamed of necking in public, unfortunately illuminated by the triangle of soft light from a streetlamp.

The cold of his wedding ring pushed against her.

She thought of her own ring, that hand and arm uncomfortably wedged between their two bodies, her married hand—the small reminder of Jules—tight against this man's crotch. She did everything in her power not to move, not to stir what began to apply pressure back against those smashed fingers, her hand not the only hardness between them.

They didn't kiss, but Kris softly moaned to make it "believable," fingers spidering through her hair because that would be visible to this woman who'd soon be upon them, and so she moved her hand slowly up and down his back. She thought of his thigh on the bus, that first touch she'd offered mostly as a dare to herself, how he'd willingly accepted that touch and had pushed back. Was it too much? Had they'd crossed over the razor's edge? A queasiness lurched in her stomach. This wasn't what she wanted. This was—

"Coming?" Kris asked barely above a whisper, breathing hot into her ear, down her neck, wet, and she almost shoved him away reflexively until she realized he meant the barista.

Chloe unburied her face from his neck, her lips, yes, they had pressed against his skin, either on purpose or not, and as inconspicuously as she could she looked around him.

The barista a few strides away.

Chloe pulled him in even closer, that useless arm of hers still wedged and acting as a barrier between their two sexes, and that was enough of an answer. She couldn't help but think about sleeping with Jules, how they'd sometimes try to snuggle in bed, and how one arm was always in the way or buried or numbed by the other's weight. This in turn recalled the time she and Jules had finished, that last time under the stars, not so long ago.

Coming.

"The fuck you doing here?"

Kris turned at the explosion of a question and pulled away. "Sorry," he said, "we just couldn't help ourselves. I mean, a night like this..."

"No, what are *you* doing *here*. You following me or something?"

"Huh?"

"You and... *Chloe*," she said, making it sound like the abomination of the spelling on the cup—*Clowy*, with an emphasis on the 'wey.' "You two, you had coffee, and now you're here? What are you doing outside my building?"

Chloe flushed at the wrongness of it all. She closed her eyes and swiveled her head, so she faced the wall, ashamed. Was it shame? She couldn't move her hand. Did she want it there? A part of her wanted to knee him in the groin and run—back to Jules. Another part of her wondered if that's what she should do, or if Kris would see it as a "Tag, you're it, catch me if you can." Had he really not done anything more after they'd parted ways that afternoon?

"Oh, this is your place?" he said, pulling fully away.

There was no use hiding anymore, Chloe exposed, she studied the ground between them, her dangling arm no longer trapped.

"Whatever," the barista said and shoved past them, taser in hand, and made her way to her car. She tossed her bag in the passenger seat, revved the engine, and sped away.

Chloe's heart hammered as the red eyes of the taillights faded into the night and blinked as they turned the corner, tires screaming.

What the hell are we doing?

"Lamest stakeout ever," she said.

Kris whistled from Nikki's stoop, foot holding the door open to the entryway.

"Ta da!" He made jazz hands. "Got to the door before it closed all the way. No longer a stakeout. More like a crime scene investigation. Time to gather evidence."

"Her crime: drive-by bitching," she said, and laughed, nerves fluttering as she ducked inside after the slightest of hesitations. Their experiment was pushing the envelope of "legal," and the tingle of fear and excitement strengthened her desire to break the rules. She was already inside; too late to turn back now.

Kris located the door he figured for Nikki's while Chloe dug through her backpack for her wallet and extracted an ancient airmiles card she should have thrown away long ago.

"Better knock first." Kris rapped on the door, and they waited, eyebrows up, ready to dash if someone answered, or give a "Sorry, wrong address, I guess."

"Nobody home," he said.

"This can't possibly work as easily as it does on those crime shows." She slid the card in next to the knob. "A little jimmy, a lot of jab, you keep pushing, jiggle that knob."

Kris bumped the door a few times as she worked the latch.

"I feel it moving," she said.

He shouldered the door harder, and it popped open.

They stood at the threshold, leaning in. "Worried?" he asked.

She was, but shook her head no.

Breaking and Entering, was that the official crime? Did it have a number? Were they a 413 or a 386 in progress?

"I guess we'd better do the 'entering' part before someone

spots us," Chloe said and lifted her foot high and took an exaggerated step. "No trip wire, no sirens. I think we're safe."

The cluttered living room merged with a rundown kitchen. Chloe studied the room, searching for motivation. What made the barista so passive aggressive? 'Nikki' surrounded herself with trappings of a proper hipster existence: record player, arty posters, thrift store treasures, even a vintage bowl full of kibble under the window. Kris went straight to the kitchen, opening and closing cupboards, laughing as he rearranged things on the fridge. He turned a magnet-backed picture upside-down, then spelled out WHAT COLOR IS THE WIND? and GOT SEX? using the primary-colored alphabet letters scattered across the grungy metal. He opened the fridge and peered inside, bit into an apple and put it back.

"What color *is* the wind?' she asked.

He took in a deep breath, let it out audibly. "*Blew.*"

Chloe thought of the crime scene shows and the clues they'd leave behind: DNA evidence, fingerprints everywhere, strands of hair and microfibers. She made a conscious effort to 'look but don't touch,' and wiped sweat from her hands onto her legs.

"She seems to be a takeout addict," he said. "Has friends, too, which is a surprise." He held out a photo of a group of women in party frocks toasting with pink martinis.

"Band of hipster-douches?" Chloe said as he stuck the photo back on the fridge. "Look at this." She pointed at a legal pad on the table, full of scribbles. A chaotic mind splashed onto the page. "She writing a novel or something?"

"Isn't everyone in a coffee shop writing a novel?"

Chloe read the last paragraph on the page. "Oh man, it's one of those riddles. Listen to this. 'I am what most fear. I strike without warning. I cannot be stopped. When uttered, I rip apart the hearts of your loved ones.' Creepy. What do you think the answer is?"

"Beats me," he said and shrugged, lost in thought.

Chloe poked him. "C'mon. Even when she's not here, bad barista is a buzz kill. I'm going to check out her bedroom, then we should head out."

In the hall, he pointed at two open doors. "She's got a roomie."

Chloe sniffed the air in both rooms. "This one smells more like ripe angst, probably hers. The other's all incense and crystals and zen," she said, then words came out on their own: "Want to vandalize?" A different 'breaking' after the 'entering.'

She found a cleanish tank top on the floor and rushed around the room, using the material to open each of the drawers, moving furniture slightly this way and that, flipping over a framed picture of the barista and who she guessed was her roomie, shuffling cosmetics bottles on top of the dresser and hangers in the closet.

Kris disappeared and reappeared with a dropper bottle of red food coloring he must have taken from the kitchen. He removed the top and squeezed as he shot an arc of blood red onto an empty white wall. "*Now* it's a crime scene," he said, happy with himself.

"Let me see that," Chloe said.

She took it to the bathroom, and he followed a little too close. After sliding the shower curtain open with a foot, she motioned for the leave-in conditioner bottle, and he grabbed it and unscrewing the cap. He held it out to her and without touching the bottle she squeezed in what was left of the red dye. He recapped, then set it back.

"You taking the tank top?" he said.

She hadn't thought of it before, but yes, she'd take it now that he mentioned it. She unballed the material and read the screen-printed words: "THE LINE BEGINS TO BLUR."

"Fuck it," she said, and peeled out of her shirt and stuffed it in her backpack along with the empty food coloring bottle.

Kris leaned against the wall and crossed his arms, watching her change.

"You badass," he said again.

She slipped on 'Nikki''s tank top.

"The line's done blurred."

"Things have definitely gone blurry," he said, and blinked dramatically.

"All right, time to go."

They went back to the living room, tilting pictures along the hall.

"Before I forget," he said, reaching into his pocket. "You got that card?" He held out a hole punch. "Found this on her roommate's desk. You at least deserve a free coffee after the way our little barista friend treated you. Treated *us*. Hand it over."

Chloe dug into her backpack for her purse, found the already filled-out card and her cheeks warmed with embarrassment, then pulled out the new one.

Thirteen flat circles of cardstock rained over the carpet.

She couldn't tell him it didn't match the punch they used at Soul.

"Let's get out of here," he said. "Spidey-senses are telling me roomie is coming homie soon. And kinda late for the 'whoops, wrong apartment' excuse."

A mewling startled them both. Slithering onto the floor through a gap in the window came one of those hideous hairless cats. She—based on the fake-diamond-bejeweled pink necklace—rubbed against Chloe's leg and sputtered a purr.

"Jesus, do pets sometimes look like their owners." Kris picked the cat up, held it like a man who's never held an infant might, by its pits. "Ugly little thing," he said with his arms straight out, "like a shriveled-up, shrunken old man. And naked." He shivered, then read the nametag on the collar. "Who names their cat 'The Void.'"

"A barista with deep, dark secrets she can only tell her freaky cat," Chloe said, scrunching her nose at the dangling animal. "Could be like a witch's familiar, and she can see us through its eyes. Let's split." Chloe shuddered as the cat turned as though to place judgment upon her.

"Wait," Kris said. "I have a crazy idea. Maybe too crazy. I can't believe I'm considering it." He set the cat on the couch and rubbed its head like one might a precocious child and unlatched the collar. "How daring you want to be?"

"What, this isn't daring?"

"Seriously, I've seen you hiding your ring. You're married, I know. And I'm married. It's obvious both of us are itching for change, so how daring do you want to be?"

Chloe flushed again and twirled the ring around her finger, both wondering what he was about to propose and remembering the night Jules had proposed... how happy they'd been, and how long ago that now seemed.

Kris made a pained face as he pulled hard at his wedding ring, and pried it round and round, over his knuckles, then held it out in his palm. "I mean, you *are* done with it all, right? I've got a plan. They're both simple enough bands, mine, yours. We'll get new ones to commemorate our liberation. Replace these before either of our 'spouses,'" he said, making air-quotes, "ever notices. Trust me?"

His expression said, *Come on*.

Coming.

She took in a deep breath and let it out slowly, then clenched her teeth as she struggled to pull the damn thing off, the ring there long enough for her body to grow around it. It choked her finger like it had choked her life for howevermany years. A simple symbolic band.

She hesitated before handing it to him and read the inscription one last time: *à jamais*. Jules had meant for it to read 'forever,' which was *toujours* if used on its own, but *son utilisation de la langue française était épouvantable*—his French so very dreadful—that she couldn't bring herself to tell him. He'd slipped it on her finger in front of all their nearest and dearest. She hadn't read the inscription until later, after resizing it because that too was wrong. So, she'd worn his mistake for the duration of their marriage.

Chloe placed it next to Kristoph's ring.

He read the inscription and smiled.

Another mistake, finger bare, exposed—

"Let's bling her up even more, shall we? An offering to The Void," he said, then unclipped the pink collar and slid it through each of the ring loops, and finally returned the collar to the cat. "May you carry our burdens and travel back to whatever gate of hell you came from."

Ringless, they snuck out of the apartment, then back onto the street.

I can't believe I'm doing this, I can't believe I'm doing this...

"Ready for the main event?" Kris said.

She was.

The building looked bigger in the dark, looming over them like an admonishing grandfather warning of unknown dangers. The emptiness around her finger itched.

"Let's find a spot back there to get in," Chloe said and let her fingers trail along the chain-link as they rounded the side of the condemned site. She pulled her hand back, worrying about fingerprints, then laughed. Unlikely she was leaving prints, and besides, who would collect evidence off a fence unless something truly terrible went down?

"Here?" Kris scanned the shadow-cloaked alley, then pulled a set of bolt-cutters from his pack. "You keep watch. I'll pretend I dropped something if anyone comes by."

"Don't worry, I got your six." Chloe stood behind him

while he cut a flap in the links. She could tell he'd never used bolt-cutters before, or hefty wire cutters, for that matter, which would have sufficed to open a fence.

A flicker of movement at the other end of the alley caught her eye. Small and pale—some kind of animal. A clink of metal on metal sounded, and whatever it was curled around a garbage can and vanished.

"Here you go." Kris held the chain-link up and she crawled through.

They ran up to the back of the building and found a plywood-covered basement window. Kris pulled a small prybar from his pack, and Chloe grabbed it.

"My turn. Otherwise, we aren't true conspirators." She jabbed the tooth-end under the plywood and levered the nail out. The board came away with a groan and she pulled a flashlight out of her bag and scanned the floor inside. "Not too far down. I'm going in."

She sat on the windowsill, then jumped. The impact sent small splinters of pain shooting up her legs, but she took a few steps and they faded. No damage. Kris landed with a grunt, then clicked on his flashlight and they took a good look at the room.

"Wonder if this place is haunted," she said.

"Yeah, not keen to be visited by the dead right now."

Something in his tone made Chloe angle her flashlight in his direction, but he turned before she could catch his expression. She wondered about his ring, how long they'd been together, and what had driven them apart. She wondered about her own ring, felt for it, but no, it wasn't there. This was all really happening. And she wondered about the next time Jules might reach for her hand and notice it missing.

A riddle from her youth: *What has hands but no arms, a face with no eyes? I point without fingers, strike without arms, run without feet. What am I?*

Time.

Was it simply time that drove couples apart? She reflexively motioned to twirl her ring again—an itch she couldn't scratch.

"Let's see what's upstairs," she said, leading the way.

A stone staircase ascended into darkness. That same tingle of excitement and fear compelled her upward.

5
Déjà vu

*S*he wanted to be needed, according to her profile, not needed to be wanted, but no, that wasn't quite right. The words in Kovelant's head were out of order, like shaking a martini with the olives, not the ice. How often were *wants* and *needs* confused with each other?

Going through the evidence brought the night back, finding all these things scattered about, eventually collected to be rediscovered in the here and now. Jigsaw puzzle pieces thrown haphazardly into a box, it seemed.

"When we die, we turn into stories," he said aloud. "What's your story?"

He pulled up to the Bisset residence minutes before noon, his stomach hungry for lunch, but his desire to find closure in the case hungrier. The coffee, his third, hit him hard, left his mind reeling and his hands shaky.

Jules Bisset opened the door to Kovelant without him needing to knock, and then led him inside.

All through the house, walls were adorned with pictures of the once-happy family. Only two included Maxie: one from what looked like Doran beach in Bodega Bay, Maxie kicking up sand next to a plastic bucket and tiny shovel, waves lapping her sandcastle, and one with the State Capitol building in the background, the trees yellowing toward fall—*Sacramento, the city of trees.* The rest: selfies of Jules and Chloe alone in sunny places, heads smashed together and smiling. Most from when they were younger. All black-and-white and artsy.

Faces smashed together, he thought, and had to shake away the image of the two fused women at the morgue.

No baby pictures of Maxie, no sweat-damp smiling new mother presenting her tiny, swaddled infant, which one would expect to find in such a once-happy home.

Had they adopted Maxie? Had they routinely swapped out family portraits for the most recent?

From what he could ascertain, the two family portraits had been taken this year. They looked staged, as though they had found pictures of themselves already featured in frames they'd purchased. One dangled crookedly on the wall, and so he straightened it as he passed by, a sprinkle of plaster falling from behind it.

He waited for Jules to say something, anything, but the man had cried out all his words. He thought of mentioning the lack of baby Maxie in the family photos.

No wonder the entire house *felt* sad. A haunting childless display of happiness; Jules surrounded by images of his dead wife, daughter at grandma's.

"This is the most recent image of her."

At first Kovelant thought he meant Maxie, but the grieving widower pointed at a photo of Chloe on the wall, touched the glass with the tip of his finger and let it stay there a moment to leave a fingerprint. He didn't look at it long, just touched it and moved on and into the kitchen, where a plated sandwich and chips and a slice of pickle awaited uneaten. He imagined the gaunt man had starved himself for days and hadn't slept for as long. Eyes shadowed in exhaustion.

Kovelant had seen a more recent photo of her, *the* most recent and final photo of Chloe Bisset, also black and white, but mostly black with death: two women who'd become one.

Tangled lives.

What surprised him was the ring on Jules's left hand, which he noticed when they both sat at opposite ends of the table: silver and smooth and nearly identical to Item #0005. He wore it on his ring finger, same as his wife.

"A lot like Chloe's," Kovelant said, pointing at the ring.

Saying her name wounded the man across from him, and he watched as Jules lifted his fingers to inspect the ring.

"Matching, in fact," he said. "When can I get hers back?"

"Soon," Kovelant promised, although it could be a long while.

Was it even hers?

The man stirred as they shared an awkward silence.

"Mind if I see it?" Kovelant said, holding out his hand.

Jules Bisset looked from the ring to the sandwich, then to the outstretched hand, and then back to the ring. He hesitated, and then pulled it free and handed it over.

New, Kovelant thought, thinking how difficult it would be to remove his own wedding ring if he tried, with years of marriage anchoring it in place for so long. Damn near impossible. This man's ring slid right off, easy-peasy. He inspected the ring—only minute scratches, like the first few dings on a new car.

"How long were you married," he asked, regretting the past-tense.

Jules snatched the sandwich, took a bite, and around a mouthful said, "Maxie's five now, so just under ten years."

Ring's younger than Maxie by the look of it.

What Kovelant wanted to ask next would be smoother after a story of his own, and so he said, "My wife and I, we hit our *twenty-third anniversary* last year. We forgot about it until a couple friends reminded us. We were out having dinner with them, nothing special, just one of those places that sells overpriced 'fancy' hotdogs," he said, making the quotes in the air with his fingers, "and saw them there, so we sat next to them. I was biting into a not-from-Chicago Dog, watching some game on the tube, and the wife of the other guy asks us, 'What are you planning for the big day?' and my wife and I both look at each other before I manage, 'Big day?' The woman says, 'Your anniversary. It's tomorrow, right?' and wouldn't you know it, it was. My wife and I, we share the same look as before and my wife goes, 'It's just another day. We don't really celebrate anniversaries and birthdays,' and I add, because it was always true, and because they were both confused, 'We've always thought *What's the point, right?* I mean, why not make *every* day count,' and my wife adds, 'If you want cake, eat cake. If you want flowers, buy flowers. If you want a week on the beach in Hawaii...' and they got it, sort of. Truth is, we had both forgotten. The date would have passed right over us had they not told us."

Sometimes you couldn't ask certain questions without frontloading. The stage was set. He could almost believe the story himself.

"We've talked a few times about doing it again," Kovelant continued, "I mean, getting married, or *re*-married, I guess. Renewing vows. Just the two of us, somewhere remote, by ourselves, maybe." He twirled Jules's ring, tossed it lightly into the air, and as it landed noticed the inscription he was looking for, though he tried to make it seem like he wasn't trying to read it. The man across from him stared blankly at the table, nothing to hide. "Ever think of renewing your vows, Mr. Bisset?"

The question was finally out there, the one he'd been meaning to ask.

Inscribed inside the ring, *séparé*, lowercase and scripty.

Kovelant maintained a neutral expression, though the word had almost made him flinch. 'Separate' was not a sentiment to inscribe on a symbol for ''til death do you part.' He'd have to look it up. A word with multiple meanings, or part of a song or poem.

"No," Jules Bisset said, with no emotion behind the word. He took another bite of his sandwich, tasteless to him, no doubt. He adjusted his glasses, thick lenses. His eyes never left the table, looking *through* the table, or at nothing at all. "Married almost ten years," he said. "Ten years next month.

Maxie will turn six soon. What am I supposed to tell her? She doesn't—"

Kovelant held out the silver ring, and the man took it and slipped it onto his ring finger as easily as he'd slipped it off. The ring was something new, and like *her* ring, held a mystery.

Free. Together. Forever, Kristoph,
séparé

"Does the name Kristoph mean anything to you?"

Jules removed his glasses and wiped them with his shirt-tail—without them his expression became vague, his face amorphous.

"Kristoph? No." He paused and thought some more. "Maybe someone from work? But no, I don't think so. Who is he?"

"A name written on something in the accident debris. Could be from the other woman's car. Could have been on site before the accident." He felt the need to protect the newly minted widower lest he shatter into pieces, at least until he knew what he was protecting the man from.

Jules Bisset's cell phone buzzed on the table, then, silenced, but not entirely, and upside-down Kovelant read the caller ID: GRANDMA L. The phone danced around before Jules acknowledged the call, and with that same empty stare answered.

"Hey Lauren... uh huh, okay," and then a pause. "Does she want to talk to me? You think she needs anything else, a ginger ale or saltines or—" he said, and then there was nothing from his end for a while, until he said, "Okay. Sure. Bring her home. Thanks."

"Everything all right?" Kovelant asked.

"Maxie threw up. Not sick, but sickened by all this, I guess. She's old enough to understand, but not old enough to grasp—"

Her mother won't be coming back.

"She wants to be with her dad?" he offered because it sounded about right.

"You have kids?"

"*Used* to," Kovelant said, the emphasized word a heavy weight, "a daughter," and that was the end of the story. A two-word story with all the ugly details left buried inside.

"We'd been talking about trying again. I asked Chloe if she wanted to go back on her vitamins, but she complained they made her queasy. Maxie really wants a little brother."

Wants, not *wanted*.

Stuck in the past.

Vodka tonic, sans the vodka, he remembered. He would have to ask Carl if there was evidence of a pregnancy.

"I wanted to check again, in case you've thought of something new. Anything unusual happen recently? Did Chloe seem worried, depressed?"

"Depressed?" Jules shook his head, but his expression seemed uncertain. "If anything, she was more active, getting back into some of her old routines from before. Running, like I said. And she was sneaking cigarettes. She'd worked so hard to quit." He shook his head again.

After a few more follow-up questions, he let Jules have his afternoon back. A sick kid took a lot out of a day, out of a person, but at least Grandma L. was there to help. Jules Bisset was lucky in that regard. Poor Maxie, now motherless. How would one ever go about explaining death to a child. *Your mother's dead, little one. Death can be cruel, Maxie. It's just you and me now, and your grandma.* Fuck, maybe he was still trying to figure out how.

Je ne sais pas comment.

I wouldn't know how either, Jules.

Kovelant and his wife had been married twenty-three years, sure, that much was true in his tale. Happily? Not that it mattered. They'd slogged through the shit all those years, each revolution around the sun more trying. The death of a parent was so much different than the death of a child. He and his better half still had both parents, in their mid-seventies and *there*, although sometimes *not entirely there*; but to lose a child, and one so young... that meant reexperiencing loss on a loop.

A knife in the gut, piercing flesh, then twisting.

Two more weeks and Lili would have made it to three. Lilikoi, they'd sometimes call her. Every June 7th, for the last twenty years, they'd celebrate her third birthday. Despite everything, they'd make time, meet at her favorite park bench. Lili forever not-quite-three. Always three candles on the small cake they'd never eat, the two of them staring upon the dancing flames as the wax dribbled down, not blowing them out—for they were not their wishes to make or destroy—and they would both watch and not cry, no, not any longer, as the candles melted to nubs as each flame snubbed out after taking a final breath. Every damn time it was like watching Lili's chest fall and never again rise.

Three, a magical number, like in the fairytales they'd read her before bed.

Kovelant had always held in his wishes of having her back, but 'wish in one hand and...' as the saying went, so what was the point?

When Lili died, she turned into a story; that's all she was now, written in his mind, a lingering *déjà vu* that always arrived unannounced. And though her pages had been reduced to ash and set on their fireplace mantle: the book of her short life took the place of future photographs, future memories. That sweet voice of hers in his mind ever-fading.

Daddy, she'd say, eyes alight, arms reaching up, *snuggle-dance time.*

He wiped tears and twirled his wedding ring like Bisset had, but unlike Bisset,' his finger had ripened with age. The ring had withstood the test of time, battered and blemished, and it would have to be snipped to be removed. He was jealous, in a way, for their daughter was still alive. Little Maxie, twice Lili's age.

Why not me? he always wondered. *Why her?*

Lili would be twenty-three now. She was one of the reasons he and Amanda had married in the first place. Not the only reason, but a big one. Kovelant tried picturing Lili as twenty-three, graduating college, or returning home with stories of backpacking adventures, but she was stuck at the age she'd died. Sometimes he'd look through his wife's old photographs to try to determine what kind of woman Lili might've become.

This Chloe Bisset case...

She had swerved into this other woman, and he wanted—*needed*—to know why she'd done so, why she'd left a daughter behind. What gave her that urge? What gave her that right? She'd killed another woman and had left a child motherless—*on purpose?*

Kovelant imagined the tires of Chloe's vehicle squealing as she pulled the steering wheel—creating those squiggly black commas on the asphalt—and the ghostly sound pulled out the worst of his memories.

Walking the streets of Sacramento was never an issue, enough one-way streets and crosswalks and signals and WALK / DO NOT WALK signs flashing to make anyone feel safe. Most intersections even audibly announced safe passage to the blind.

"Want to keep going?" Kovelant said, his idea, not hers.

Amanda smiled and nodded, pushing the stroller ahead of them. Lili had often lifted her arms into the air to be picked up and carried after only a few blocks or so, hence the stroller. It was a wonderfully crisp Sunday morning, the sun ducking between fat battleship clouds, city life not yet hustling and bustling with the brunch crowd.

They'd started at H Street and 11th and took their time as they reached the Capitol building to walk through its rose garden. One specimen of every tree in the state surrounded them, each with a placard announcing their biological genera and common name, and they stopped at the ones flowering to take in their aromas. For this second wind of their walk, they bought lattes at a local roaster called Temple, and were off to explore a deeper downtown. Kovelant pulled out a flask of whiskey to make their drinks 'special,' a weekend tradition of theirs.

"I've never been past U Street," she said.

"Me neither, not on foot. Lots of abandoned buildings."

"You'd think they'd just tear some of these down after a while, windows broken out and whatnot. Fire hazards, no doubt. These are *old* buildings," she said, emphasizing the word and touching the early gray hairs on his beard. "All brick on the outside, all soft on the in—"

He slowed to light a cigarette.

Neither heard the Prius until tires screeched around the corner, clipping the front left wheel of the stroller, enough to send it tumbling down the sidewalk in a spin, Lili asleep, tossed out ragdoll-like, flopping across the cement and into the side of a refuse bin. He'd never forget that sound. Amanda was pulled with the stroller, and she'd first held on, her maternal-reflex instincts kicking in, perhaps, which yanked and crumpled her across the hood, shattering the windshield with her body, special coffee splashing everywhere.

Despite three later-diagnosed broken ribs, left collar bone, ulna, she somehow got to Lili before he could and fell on her knees next to her.

Kovelant's quick-processing mind shattered in that moment. His lighter and smoke fell from numb fingers. He stared at his daughter's limp form—so much like a toy—then at his wife, and at the traumatized and horrorstricken face in the Prius. The driver stopped long enough to sear that image into Kovelant's mind, a kid no older than sixteen, drove off like the coward he was.

He couldn't manage a plate number, couldn't manage any normal function until his wife called out in desperation.

"John!"

He blinked and ran to her side. Amanda held Lili in her arms, one hand cradling her shattered skull, life seeping out between fingers.

Lili, little Lilikoi, breathed in, breathed out, and it was her last.

To this day, he could only recall the kid's face. The car might not have even been a Prius, dubbed the silent killers by those at the station for their lack of engine-noise. He'd registered some ugly wedge-shaped thing. They'd never found the driver. Hit and Run. This was before smart phones. Before cameras at every intersection. Before technology made it more difficult to hide from crime.

Kovelant would put these pieces together in the Bisset case. He was determined to at least figure out motive. There had to be a reason. The traffic camera footage would reveal something, which is what he found himself thinking as he sat down with the station's tech guy.

"What did you find?" Kovelant asked.

"It's black-and-white because of the hour of the recording, and a bit fuzzy and pixilated in the darker areas, but she's here," he said, pointing to Chloe Bisset's Ford Explorer, no larger than a pinky nail on the large monitor. "I've queued it up and cleaned up the image as much as technology allows, but this is your driver," he said and tapped the screen. "Zoom in too much and it makes it tough to see what happens."

My driver, Kovelant thought, and once again the twenty-year image of the hit-and-run driver was there, as though he'd never left, having only been placed into a file and pulled out every so often to hurt.

The video, from an overpass, looked down upon the freeway. Blurry and pixilated as all get out, but there she was, Chloe Bisset. Paused and alive at this moment. Her Ford Explorer had once been some shade of silver according to the Department of Motor Vehicles, but appeared white on the screen, and in the distance was Sue Montgomery's smudge of black Volkswagen. Each in their lanes heading the opposite direction. One lit the road with headlights, the other trailed taillights, captured in the very moment before impact.

Time displayed on the bottom left of the video, and Kovelant noted it, which matched the estimates. Both women out late. Hardly any other vehicles on the freeway. Because of construction—repaving and an additional lane— there was no barrier, only plastic pylons to keep drivers on the right path, dotting the center divide every so often.

"This is a nasty one," the tech said.

"Estimated speeds?"

"I'd guess Montgomery was going around fifty, fifty-five, typical freeway speeds during construction, but Bisset here was going faster, maybe sixty, seventy. Tough to tell, but faster by at least ten or twenty. I've watched this thing a hundred times and—"

"Show me," Kovelant said, but not unkindly.

The tech hit a button and the video was over in a breath: two vehicles in their respective fast lanes, suddenly becoming one in Montgomery's lane after a quick dance. They watched the video a half-dozen times before Kovelant asked him to play it slower.

At a tenth the speed, the two vehicles jutted toward each other, a tease of what would soon happen. The same uncomfortable anticipation built with every viewing. Both stayed in their lanes until just before the end, before Chloe Bisset's Explorer swerved last-second hard and to the left, crossing the makeshift center divide, and entering the other lane, then straightening again.

"You've gotta be kidding me," Kovelant said.

"Strange, right?"

Not only had the French woman swerved into the other lane, but she corrected so that they'd hit head-on. The cars were not perfectly in alignment, but the women were. Chloe Bisset not trying to swerve back, but purposefully setting her car straight. All in a fraction of a second. And just after the crash, the vehicles clung together and spun to a stop counterclockwise across multiple lanes of empty freeway.

Two vehicles becoming one.

Two women becoming one.

"Homicide."

"Looks like."

6
The Experiment: Testing the Prediction

A series of wooden doors both welcomed and unwelcomed them, some open, some closed. Angled wood planks of the exposed subfloor pricked with a stubble of flooring nails.

"Do you know what this building was?" Kris said and played his flashlight's beam up and down the hall.

"I was going to look it up but thought figuring it out would be more fun." Chloe shone her flashlight along the hall in the other direction. "Shit, what's that?"

A silhouette broke up an expanse of plastered wall, long and lumpy.

Kris trained his light on the dark figure, then on another, further down.

Chloe laughed when she realized what they were looking at. "It's just holes in the plaster. Probably from salvaging copper wire."

Kris let out a shaky breath.

Her hand appeared pale and bloated in her flashlight beam as she pushed open one of the doors. A room with boarded windows. Office? Hotel room? Dorm? She moved to the next door, a double set, pushed them open. Some sort of chapel? She pointed her light to the end of the room where a few steps led up to a lectern, the wooden base gouged and listing. The floor had scars where pews were once screwed down.

"I'm thinking church or Catholic school," he said.

Chloe opened the door across the hall.

"The hell is *that?*"

A pile of grade-school desks rose from the middle of the room, legs bristling out spider-like in all directions.

She remembered slouching over similar desks, scribed with initials and declarations from their former occupants. "Well, that answers it."

"So. We're here. What did you want to do?" Kris turned to Chloe and held his flashlight under his chin, his mouth a shadow-grin and his eyes black holes.

Chloe shrugged. "I mean, at this point I expected all our efforts would have, I dunno, changed something. But I feel the same. It's just me, out here in the middle of the night, in an abandoned building."

"And me."

She pictured Jules snoring on his side of the bed, unaware the other side had long emptied and cooled, and Maxie, face down, butt up, thumb jammed tight in her mouth, her breath sweetened by ice cream flavored toothpaste.

Abandoned.

"We could try to force the issue. Make things blur, like it says on your top." His light moved to her chest.

She really didn't want to go where she thought he was suggesting. Infidelity didn't feel like a dare, like a liberation from the mundane. Cheating was a cliché. And in the movies, every time a woman stepped over that line, all hell rained down, whereas the guy got nothing more than some crank calls and a boiled rabbit for his troubles.

"Look, I—" she said.

Kris dropped his light and pulled three metal cylinders from his pack. Two with red caps—spray paint? The third a thermos or flask.

"It's confession time. But first, some liquid courage." He opened the flask and offered it; woody-sweet whiskey fumed out. A cheap brand.

"What are we confessing?"

"Our deepest darkest secret, our hidden desires, the worst thing we never want to admit to the world or to ourselves." He brought the flashlight back to his chin and his shadow-grin leered. "You remember the barista's latest riddle?"

"Something like *I am what you fear and can't be stopped. I rip apart the hearts of your loved ones.*" Chloe considered. "The truth; it tears everything apart."

"And will set you free, as they say. Time to share those painful secrets."

Chloe took a slug of whiskey, coughed, then took two more. A fiery parasite curling inside her belly. She handed the flask over and said, "I'm boring. I don't have secrets."

"Does a boring person raise the roof in front of the 7-11?

Would a boring person be here, tonight?" Kris tapped her forehead with one of the spray cans, then placed it in her hand. "Let's spray our truths on the wall." Kris turned and went back into the chapel.

"Okay," Chloe said, "but no peeking. You take that wall; I'll take this one."

She set her flashlight on the stripped subfloor and studied her wall: cracked plaster with lathe and brick showing through in places, time-darkened outlines where crucifixes and portraits of saints and virgins must have hung. She glanced at Kris, and he glanced back.

"I said no looking."

"Yeah, yeah," he said, "but you've gotta dig. Write the dark, awful, terrible truth."

Chloe took a deep breath and closed her eyes. She pictured her life, her family. Everything done in order: marriage, job, house, baby. The portraits she'd hung— each a display of happiness, togetherness, the perfect family. *Joie de vivre*. That's the story the pictures told. But it wasn't true.

She thought back to the last time she was happy. A Hard-Core Logo concert years ago, holding hands with Jules in the mosh pit, grinning up at the stage, sweat plastering their hair, the way his t-shirt clung to him made her want to slide her hands up under, merge with him, never let him go. As the band launched into their ballad, "Blue Tattoo," he pulled her in for a slow dance and yelled in her ear, "You are inked on my soul."

She'd felt alive, then, and wanted, *needed*.

They'd gone to the beach a few months back, with a blanket and a bottle of wine, and it was nice. But forced.

The cap came off the spray can with a pop, and as she shook it the little thing inside rattled. A stuttering hiss came from behind her—Kris's confession.

Chloe pushed down on the nozzle and pictured her daughter. Maxie's gap-toothed smile. Feather-light hair. Tiny, ribbed fingers worming into everything. Her laugh a gurgle of lunatic glee. She graffiti'd her confession:

I DON'T WANT TO BE A MOTHER!

The words bled.

She placed a shaking hand on her stomach.

Raised the can again, heart pounding.

She needed to erase the confession, make it not true.

Red streaming down.

"Ready or not," Kris said, his paint can clattering to the floor. "Time for show and tell, *mon amour*."

Chloe turned, and it took her a moment to decipher Kris's confession. His words arced down the wall, large misshapen letters in a drunken slant:

I WANT TO KILL MY WIFE.

"What the fuck?" Chloe stepped back and kicked her flashlight, the beam spinning around, light pulsing, shadows warping.

Kris wiped his nose and laughed. "Yeah, I picked the wrong phrasing, but once I started, I had to just go for it. I can't bring myself to leave her and can't stand the idea of her leaving me. I mean, don't you ever wish someone were, I don't know, *gone?*"

Yes, gone.

Chloe's flashlight settled on her wall, and he read her truth. "Ah. I see you do."

"Not like that." Chloe sank to her knees. "Not dead."

"No? Then how?"

"I don't know."

"It's an important question, right? One of the fundamentals. Well, while you think about it, nature calls." Kris grabbed his pack and left the chapel.

She loved Jules. She loved her daughter, too. But her life felt hollow, or *she* felt hollow. After Maxie was born, doctors told her it was post-partem depression. They gave her pills—serotonin-reuptake inhibitors, a low dose at first, then upped as she spiraled down—and that helped. So did time. But the feeling never went away.

I'm a bad person. Chloe wiped her face, then held out her hand, fingers tacky and red. *You did this. It can't be me.*

A new smell wafted into the room: fuel.

Yellow-orange light flickered from the classroom a few doors down when she stepped into the hall. She rushed to that doorway.

"What are you doing?"

Kris grinned from the other side of the burning mountain of desks, his eyes bright with reflected flame. "This is it, Chloe. The first step. We confess, and the fire cleanses."

"We've got to put it out! What if it spreads? What if there's someone in the building? Jesus." Chloe scanned the room, looking for anything that might help. A curtain. An extinguisher. Overhead pipes or fire sprinklers. Any source of water.

Kris held his hands out as though warming them over a campfire. "How do you propose to put it out? With your thermos of hot chocolate?"

She removed her hoodie and beat the fire, and the fabric caught after fanning the flames, so she tossed it in. The heat overwhelmed. She stepped back, dumfounded, in the stolen tank top. *The line begins to blur.*

"We've got to get out of here." Chloe skirted the growing blaze and grabbed his sleeve. "This place is bone dry. What the fuck are you thinking?" She pushed Kris in front of her. "Run, you idiot. The second someone sees smoke the fire department and cops'll be all over us."

They raced down to the basement. Chloe was sure embers would rain on them as they retraced their steps to the open window, but only a whisper of smoke had found its way down. She dragged an old washtub and flipped it upside down and they clambered up and out. The chain-link raked her back and jangled as she ducked through and ran around the building and out to the street, Kris close behind. Both coughing out smoke.

"Shit. *Stop!*" She held out her arm, but it was too late.

Nikki, the barista, stood next to her car, mouth open as smoke billowed from the upper floor. *You.* Her lips formed the word, then she jumped in her car and revved the engine.

"What the hell is she doing here?" Chloe said as the barista's taillights blinked out when the car screeched around a corner.

"She must have followed us from her building," Kris said, and laughed. "Looks like we're not the only ones playing games."

"She's going to call the cops. *Fuck.*" Chloe pictured the headline: MIDDLE-CLASS MOM ON FIERY LATE-NIGHT RAMPAGE. Vandalism, breaking and entering, and who knew what else. "What are we going to do?"

"Finish what we started," Kris said, and gripped her shoulders. "We've taken the first step. Now we just have to figure out how to go the rest of the way."

"What are you talking about? What steps? The rest of the way to *where?*"

"Liberation. Realization of our inner truth." Kris's fingers dug into her shoulders as his face loomed closer. "It's too late. We need to finish this."

7

Jamais vu

"K ovelant," he said, answering his cell phone. Carl again, from the caller ID, but he always answered the same. With luck, Carl was calling with another piece of the puzzle, a corner—from a coroner. So far what they had was a box of many pieces, none of which fit together but somehow would eventually create a distinguishable picture. And there was a pause on the other end of the line, which meant it would be something good, something worth his time.

"Hey, John. Thought I'd give you another ring."

"Did you find something else?"

"You know I never *find* anything," he said. "I'm only ever *brought* what ends up on my table, what's already found. But seriously, another ring, sort of."

"On whose body, Bisset's, or our mystery woman?"

"Neither. A Jane Doe came in this morning, found underneath the Discovery by an older couple bloating ducks with bread. Possibly a jumper, but odd circumstances."

The Discovery Park Bridge wasn't ever more than twenty or so feet above the water, but the Sacramento River was at a low point, last he checked driving the I-5 into downtown. He often walked the trails there, had crossed that bridge for the view and for fresh air, taking in the modest cityscape. By 'jumper,' Carl had not meant suicide, but thrill-seeker. The city was in the middle of repainting the bridge its awful-eyesore green, and so college kids used that opportunity of the barriers being down to dare each other to toss themselves over the railing. Only ten or so feet deep at most, he figured, the water murky because of the drought and lack of snowmelt from the Sierra Nevadas, though the homeless still bathed there.

"She hit one of the rocks?"

"With her face, unfortunately."

"She young?"

"We'd certainly think so. Mid-thirties, maybe younger."

So no, not some kid being a kid, but a woman wanting to be a kid again, unless she'd purposefully aimed for the rock. Kovelant set up the scene, imagined the woman leaning out over the railing, that moment of "Should I do it?" baiting her. *Yes, do it.* Someone had to have been with her if it were an accident. Thrill-seeking often requires voyeurs. But he couldn't imagine a spectator either up there with her or at the shoreline coaxing her to jump. Would've seen the rock from either perspective.

"Broken bones?"

"Her face," he repeated casually, "head cracked like a melon."

"I mean her legs, specifically, or any other injuries on her body."

"Nothing but the cranium. They found her face-down, feet on the shore as though partially dragged there, the rest of her body submerged. Hence the 'odd' in the circumstances. I'm still working on her, but her lungs were full—water and silt, so she'd stayed like that overnight—and the official cause of death will be *respiratory impairment from submersion*. Drowning. She survived the fall and would have lived if not for the river, and if someone had found her earlier. But dragged semi-out of the water, so..."

"What about the ring?"

"This is where odd turns into strange. I said there was a ring, *sort of*. She wasn't wearing one but *had* worn a wedding ring until recently. The water swelled her body, sure, but there's a ring line where a real one used to be—an indentation, or *ghost* ring, you could say. Wouldn't have taken much effort to remove it, but the mark is there. Serious tan line."

This all seemed so familiar, yet new. The opposite of *déjà vu*, a new memory that's not a memory sparked by an older one. The collision—not only of the two charred women tangled together but this latest information—was not an accident, but something much more. They were connected, these two cases.

A flash of the fused bodies of Chloe Bisset and Ms. Montgomery surged, and he blinked until the apparition faded.

"Kovelant?"

"Yeah, I'm still here. Just absorbing connections,

disconnections, endless possibilities. Let me know if you find anything more about this new Jane Doe."

"Sacramento Sheriff already ran prints. Nothing. No record. And no one's claimed her. They're checking missing persons now, but you know how that goes. Lots of names, lots of reports, but seldom anything out of it. Needles and haystacks and all that."

"Dental records?"

"Already on it."

"What are the chances Chloe Bisset might have been pregnant?" he asked, saying the thought that had plagued his mind aloud. "Can you tell from the mess you're working with? You understand what I'm asking." The second part was not a question but needed an answer.

"With time," the coroner said.

"Keep me posted."

He hung up without a salutation, same as always, and cringed inside.

Carl must think I'm a goddamn prick.

Kovelant spent the rest of the afternoon combing through evidence. Each bag held something, yes, but whether or not *that* something was relevant to the case was uncertain. There had to be a reason his team had spent all hours of the night and early morning bagging and tagging. It was always some small thing that turned out to be important, often hidden in the numbers.

EVIDENCE

Agency: Sacramento County Sheriff's Department

Collected by: John Kovelant

Item #: 0027   **Case #:** 2019-08249273

Date: 04/15/19   **Time:** 03:59

Description: Punch card for Soul (alley coffee shop in mid-town), thirteen holes punched.

Location: Chain-link fence (same as items 0014 - 0028)

Remarks: Free coffee next visit!

He couldn't remember writing the line about the free coffee, but it was late, or rather early at the time of collection, a little before four, so he was loopy and in need of coffee himself. He smiled. Even in the direst of situations, he'd found something to take the edge off. Humor needed horror, and vice versa.

The punch card was filled out, which might mean something, maybe not. The free coffee came at the fourteenth visit, not the thirteenth. Why not an even dozen? This made him wonder who made the coffee back at the station, the pot always half-full or half-empty, however you wanted to look at it. Kovelant drank three or four cups each day, sometimes more, but he never made it, didn't even know where they kept the coffee filters, nor knew the brand of bean.

EVIDENCE

Agency: Sacramento County Sheriff's Department

Collected by: John Kovelant

Item #: 0028   **Case #:** 2019-08249273

Date: 04/15/19   **Time:** 04:07

Description: Black cardstock, business card size, white text with a riddle.

Location: Chain-link fence (same as items 0014 – 0028)

Remarks: WTAF?

Kovelant read the riddle aloud, as he had the night/morning of the accident. "'I have no hands, but knock on your door, sometimes quiet, sometimes loud. You rarely know when I pass you by, but if you catch me, you might fly.'" He repeated a few of the lines, shaking his head. He sucked at riddles. The only one he knew was 'What month has twenty-eight days?' *All of them.* And 'What question can you never answer 'yes' to?' *Are you asleep?*

Then he vocalized his own new riddle, a single word. "Soul?"

Arachnid, he'd first thought, or maybe Carl Hogan

had placed that disturbing visual in his mind, but why the familiarity, past or present? And then he remembered, as though for the first time: Michael Knight; not the guy from the 80's show with the talking car, but the poet.

Kovelant had always arranged his books alphabetically by last name, so he found the book right after a few Stephen King detective novels.

Sifting the Ashes, the book was called.

He flipped to the table of contents, and there it was, on page 196.

ARACHNID

> *There's news of a couple,*
> *found one atop the other,*
> *ribs intertwined, was said,*
> *died heart-to-heart,*
> *breast-to-chest,*
> *discovered in, the paper read,*
> *their master bedroom;*
> *two bodies melded,*
> *skulls fused,*
> *torsos conjoined,*
> *metacarpals curled*
> *round one another*
> *into amalgamated fists,*
> *and their last pelvic kiss*
> *would last forever,*
> *it was said, true love.*

Perhaps he was trying to save her;
or maybe the other way around;
could be he died inside her,
coming with the fire.

The transmogrified body,
it was reported, had turned black,
like the dog remains
found curled by the door,
perhaps watching;
their eight appendages akimbo,
a dead spider
smashed flat,
such a vile-looking thing,
never seen anything like it,
the coroner had said,
or so the paper read,
this poor couple,
two becoming one;
but death serves them right,
says the surviving widow.

True love. The stories similar, but not quite: a burned home instead of a traffic collision; two women instead of a man and a woman; smashed flat instead of tarantula-curled around one another. Two becoming one. Eight appendages akimbo. A surviving widow in both stories.

Jesus.

Discovery Park was how he'd expected to find it. Yellow caution tape. A forensics team combing the litter-heavy, sandy-pebble beach. Onlookers. Everyone's breath mock-smoking in the cold. Sac. County Sheriff still milled about, hands in pockets and sipping coffees. There were drag marks by the shore, either from removing the body or from the impression Jane Doe had made while the water lapped and tasted her all night. In the shallow water directly beneath the middle of the bridge was the rock she'd hit. A splotch of red paint marked the impact, still wet. She must have seen the rock, for the moon had been three-quarters full. The rock would have stood out white against the black of the water.

Need coffee. Something strong.

"What can I get you?" the barista asked, although the twenty-something-year-old didn't seem entirely interested. He had a face that screamed of familiarity; an old soul which was fitting for the place. Comfortable with his femininity, tired from a long shift. Kovelant knew the feeling, wondering about the last time he'd slept.

He slid the filled-out punch card across the counter. "The free one," he said, "you claim that on the next visit, or when punched?"

He regretted the last word the moment he said it, for the barista startled and his chest contracted, protective. He sharpened when he spotted Kovelant's badge. Clearly shy of authority figures. Were old bruises hiding under those deep-set eyes, or pulling out blue from lack of sleep? He couldn't help but imagine both scenarios, stereotyping a natural part of the job.

"Depends," the barista said. "Technically there *is* no thirteen?"

"No?"

An unpunched card moved across the counter. The small print in lucky slot number thirteen: FREE. On Bisset's card—the word had been punched clean through.

"Like elevator buttons," he explained to Kovelant, then rotated the card ninety degrees. The punch slots in fact resembled elevator buttons, and the card itself a building flipped on its side. "Most buildings skip the thirteenth floor." And then added in a fake-happy, rambled-it-off-countless-times tone, "Here at *Soul*, we're just as superstitious. Our customers never pay for drink thirteen. It doesn't exist, right, so why should you pay for it?"

"I noticed you aren't wearing a nametag," Kovelant said. "You new?"

"Not new, no. I've worked here three years."

"What's your name?"

"Michelle."

"Like the French *Michel?*"

"Two l's, two e's. I identify as female."

He nodded, trying not to seem taken aback, embarrassed for asking about the name. Another long-time habit he'd been trying to break over the years, like smoking.

"Nice to meet you, Michelle. I'm Detective Kovelant."

The chipper smile disappeared, although she seemed more comfortable now that the pronoun was cleared up. "But that card's no good. I can get you a free coffee 'cause of your badge though. We're supposed to do that."

"The free coffee card expired or something?"

"They don't expire. I'm not saying *you* did it, but whoever punched that card doesn't work here. That's from a regular hole-punch like you'd get from a department or office supply store." She reached under the counter again and grabbed her own hole punch and *snicked* the new card, killing the first slot, making a little ☙ symbol. "It's supposed to be steaming and percolating coffee beans, but to me it looks like an asshole under a tramp stamp taking a shit. Sorry, can't unsee that now. You want a light, medium, or dark roast? Light has more caffeine, dark more flavor. The medium roast is most popular."

"Light, then."

She turned her head to the man-bun with the tattoos at the espresso machine and said, "Can I get a light roast for a cop? Detective, I mean," addressing Kovelant.

"That doesn't mean he's going to spit in it, right?"

The barista smirked and said, "No, but that's good. Just means 'large.'" She returned to her happy-fake voice: "Here at Soul, we respect first responders as well as all those in uniform, so this one's on the house." Then in a flat voice: "Can I get you anything else? Donut?"

More comfortable around him now.

"You have donuts?"

"A joke. We have bagels; close enough, right?"

"Cupa' joe is fine," Kovelant said, reaching for the coffee, looking around the place. He wanted to smoke an entire carton of Marlboros and imagined Chloe Bisset at this counter at some point. He then recalled the mangled bodies still smoking and the urge to turn his lungs into scorched lumps quickly passed. His hand knocked against an antique glass bowl with a sign sticking out of it.

CONUNDRUMS FOR THE CURIOUS. DON'T TAKE ONE.

The same white text on black cardstock as the riddle in his pocket.

"What happens if I take one?"

"It says not to. Some souls aren't meant to be broken."

"Curiosity killed the cat, something like that?"

"They're just riddles," she said and shrugged. There was no one behind Kovelant, but she looked over his shoulder anyway.

"But what might I find in these conundrums?"

"Darkness," she said flatly.

"Just going to borrow one." The papers rustled together as he made his selection. "'The more of this there is, the less you see,'" Kovelant read aloud.

"*See?*"

The answer *was* darkness. So, the barista knew the cards, then, probably all of them. Both the non-questions and their answers, if that's what they could be called. Can there be an answer if there is no question? Another conundrum.

Don't take one, he thought and put it back.

"What happens if I *give* one?"

94

Kovelant pulled the riddle from his pocket and placed it on the counter. "'I have no hands, but knock on your door, sometimes quiet, sometimes loud. You rarely know when I pass you by, but if you catch me, you might fly.'"

She startled again, shrinking away from him, or the card. Then she shrugged again.

"I don't know that one."

"No?"

The bell over the door jingled, but it was someone leaving, and so he continued his questioning. He held up a picture of what Chloe Bisset used to look like. She and her husband Jules stood in front the border sign leading into Oregon with little Maxie squinting into the sun. WELCOME TO OREGON, the sign read. He'd pulled the image off Facebook. He imagined the three of them standing on the other side of the sign: WELCOME TO CALIFORNIA, or NOW LEAVING OREGON, or whatever that side read. Kovelant had never left California in all his years of detective work. Barely left Sacramento.

"Have you seen this woman?"

"I see hundreds of people coming through here each day, but I tend to work the later shifts. She looks familiar, but not. Brack," she said, turning to the hair-bun at the espresso machine. "Seen this woman before?"

Man-bun walked over and thoughtfully took in the image. "Nah," he said, "but I'm usually the one making drinks and calling out names. They don't let me work the counter because I'm bad with handling change. And probably this." He pointed at his neck to the colorful hummingbird sucking foam from a cappuccino. Dedicated to his craft.

"The name Chloe Bisset ring a bell?"

"Chloe, yeah, I remember the name and the drink. Quad-shot, half-sweet vanilla latte. The face doesn't look familiar, though. Hold on, let me check with Sammi. She's at the front counter more than anyone. Hey Sam—"

A woman restocking boxes of K-cups gave Kovelant a head-tilt as she approached the counter. Again, the badge. "Yeah, what's up?"

"Recognize her?"

He held up the photo, and there was something in the young woman's eyes, a sparkle, but only for a moment, a reflection of the overhead fluorescents. And the smallest curl from one side of her mouth that could have been a smile, a cringe, or a tic.

She wore a nametag: Nikki.

"I thought your name was Sam?" he said.

"Oh this?" she said, looking down. "A running joke. Someone named Nikki used to work here before this place was even called Soul. When she left—*fired*—she turned in her nametag all stoic like and slammed it on the counter. We swap our tags and take turns wearing this one to confuse the guy who owns this place. He's called everyone Nikki at some point. Even Brack."

"What about her?" he said and flicked his head to the photo.

"Quad-shot, half-sweet vanilla latte," she said.

Kovelant's phone buzzed in his pocket, then, as if on cue. He swore under his breath, about to put it on Silent, but he recognized the Caller ID.

"Hold on," he said to the young woman. "I have a few more questions for you." He handed her the photograph, but she looked past the dead woman and her surviving family to the riddle on the counter. Another sparkle. "Kovelant," he said into his cellular, same as always. Another habit he'd never break. He took a long and too-hot sip of his coffee and let it burn his throat, then cleared it. "Give me something good, Carl."

"I have a name," the coroner said. "Our Jane Doe from the river. Believe it or not, her name is *not* Jane Doe. Sorry, bad joke. Dental records belong to a Mrs. Julia Freemont. Husband is Kristoph Freemont. *Kristoph*. Same spelling as the inscription on Chloe Bisset's ring. And yes, before you ask, I already have an address and contact number for you."

He dialed the number on his way to the Freemonts', GPS taking him the fastest route. He lost count of the number of times he tried to call, but it kept going to voicemail: "Hi, you've reached Julia Freemont. I'm not close enough to my cell—I managed to escape. Get it, *cell*, as in we're all prisoners of our phones, am I right?—so try me again or leave a message."

She was dead, but kept alive digitally, what remained of her stuck in some binary cloud. Digital purgatory. Mrs. Freemont's haunting yet inviting voice said to keep trying, though, and so he did, like a stalker. Finally, an answer, testing the small speaker with far too many decibels to come through clearly.

"Who's this?"

"I'm calling about Julia Freemont."

"Who's this and why do you keep calling?"

"I have a few questions and would like to schedule a meeting?"

"Look, I only answered because you've called twenty or so times in a row and I wanted to tell you personally to fuck off. Call again and I'll report you to the authorities. Do you understand? You're not a contact in this phone, so—"

"No, I'm most assuredly not. Is this Julia Freemont's phone?"

"She doesn't take sales calls. Not interested."

"This isn't—"

The call ended with a beep, then silence. He called again. Had the right number, at least, and knew in his gut it was Kristoph Freemont on the other line. His wife was dead, and someone kept calling her phone, so of course he'd be a little upset. Yet his choice of tense told a certain tale. 'She *doesn't* take sales calls,' he'd said, as though still alive.

The husband would have known about her death by now, would have confirmed the identity of her body.

Kovelant could picture the man's face, the police sketch already charcoaling itself in his mind. Mid-thirties, no older than late-twenties. Chin stubble against the phone, the cause of some of the scratchiness of the call.

The call rang twice, then died; no voicemail, which meant he'd ignored the call. And so Kovelant called again, and then a third time.

"Look, you stupid piece of shi—"

"You're speaking with Detective Kovelant from the Sacramento County Sheriff's Office. Now, I'd appreciate it if you'd not hang up this time. I'd like to schedule a meeting to discuss Julia Freemont, and I'd like that meeting to be in the next few minutes. Is this Kristoph?"

After a moment of silence, Kovelant pulled the phone away from his ear. The call had ended prematurely again. The next time he called, it went straight to voicemail.

A quick call the station to check—no one had gone in to identify Julia Freemont.

He threw his phone to the seat next to him and kept driving, took a long sip of coffee and let it burn his throat. Hot as the coffee.

8
Results: Analysis of Data

Chloe wasn't surprised to see Kris on the bus. She was surprised she hadn't seen him sooner. He sat four seats back, by the window, a grizzled old guy in classic hobo-wear next to him. They could have been friends, equally unkempt and vacant. Kris stared out the window, a week's worth of stubble descending into the stretched-out neck of his T-shirt. Had he seen her? He gave no indication.

They needed to talk. But a thick worm of dread seeped outward from Chloe's stomach, her limbs heavy and tired. She'd taken up running again. Had to after Jules woke that first night to find her in the shower early, soaping away dust, smoke, and guilt. It was strange how easy it was to deceive her husband. He didn't notice the circles that darkened under her eyes with each sleepless night, how clumsy she'd become, every sudden noise causing her to drop or bump or tip something. Maxie noticed and made a game of it. Each time mommy dropped something, she'd laugh and toss something else on the floor.

How had Jules not noticed her bare finger? She rubbed the spot where her wedding ring used to be, had rubbed it enough to make the skin tender.

From the way Kris was dressed, he clearly wasn't on his way to work. So, he must have come to talk to her. His gaunt cheeks and hollow eyes reflected in the bus window stirred another wave of dread.

Chloe got off the bus two stops after the coffee shop. She'd taken to drinking the crap coffee in the staff room even though 'Nikki' hadn't turned them in, it seemed. In the paper the fire had been attributed to a homeless man who authorities said squatted in the area and whose cook fires had caused problems before. So far, they hadn't located the man, and Chloe stared at the ceiling some nights certain that they'd find him in that building, charred and stiff, his eyes melted away and rats feasting on his crisped flesh. Other nights she remembered what she'd written, and Kris's parting words.

We need to finish it.

A quick text to the office to let them know she was running late, and Chloe headed for the cemetery. No need to look back; she knew Kris followed. The sun burned through the morning haze, and by the time she settled on a bench, sweat trickled down her back.

"Fancy meeting you here," Kris said with forced joviality.

She made herself smile and said, "Just like old times."

A cloud of sparrows lifted from the construction crane

across the street, and Chloe held her breath until they billowed away. No, not going to follow them this time.

Kris scratched his chin. "So. How're things?"

"Things are"—it was time for truth—"*fucked*, really. I can't do anything the normal way anymore. I try, but I can't. I get an impulse, and I do that instead. A reflex."

Kris nodded. "I quit my job. Just walked backward out of the office, both middle fingers in the air and yelled 'Smell ya later, fuckers.'"

Chloe laughed. "I've always wanted to do that. And I like my job. Jules asked what was for dinner last night and I threw a stack of takeout menus at him. He thought it was funny. Wasn't meant to be. He loved it when Maxie refused to let me dress her, so I took off my clothes and we watched cartoons, even joined us in his skivvies. I go for a run every morning now. But I'll see a cat dart into a yard and next thing I know I'm jumping a fence, tearing through someone's hedge. I almost got bit by a freaking Labradoodle the other day."

"But it feels good, right? You feel free?"

"I feel out of control. Scared." Chloe clasped her arms over her chest and closed her eyes. "And yet, I don't have to agonize anymore, to worry if I'm doing the right thing, making the right choice. I'm just along for the ride. Addicted to spontaneity."

"Are you ready to see where it takes you?"

Chloe shook her head, but she didn't pull away, didn't leave.

He fumbled in his pocket and pulled out three rings and said, "Here," and peered inside the bands, "these are yours."

The rings glinted in the morning sun. A men's band, polished bright and new, the women's dulled by time.

"Why two rings for me?"

"A chance to sever the bond."

Chloe took the rings and strained to read the inscriptions. *Free. Together. Forever, Kristoph,* on the smaller one, and *séparé* in a lowercase script on the bigger, which could mean either separated or apart.

She considered her old ring, which they'd offered to the cat—to The Void—and with à jamais etched in a slightly similar font. Together they read: à jamais *séparé.* Finally, apart.

The message loud and clear.

"I thought it would say something about blurring the line," Chloe said.

Kris held up his ring and slid it onto his finger. "We've done that and more."

She mirrored him and then spun the ring until her skin warmed the metal. At least now her hand felt complete. She tucked the extra ring in her purse.

"I'm guessing there'll be some things in the news," he said. "I've already done what I needed to. You'll know what you must do. How to finally be free."

He stood and retreated a few steps, smiling, that mischievous spark back in his eyes, then he pulled up his hood and turned away.

9
Non Concluant

Kristoph Freemont wasn't at the address Carl had provided, but Kovelant placed a call in to Sac. Sheriff to report what he knew about the Freemont death, and what he suspected of these two now-linked cases. Chloe Bisset was dead, found wearing a ring with Kristoph Freemont's name engraved inside the band. Julia Freemont was dead, and now he had a missing ring.

What the Sam Hell? as his mother used to say, trying not to swear, but failing.

And what did Sue Montgomery have to do with this information orgy, or was she collateral damage from whatever was going on between these two couples? *Menage a quatra*, was that a thing? *Quatuor;* that was the phrase for foursome. He'd remembered that from college days, when one of his roommates had insisted there was something beyond a *menage a trois*. Strange how some memories stick more than others. It had nothing to do with sex.

Inconclusive; that's what all this was now, this confusion.

Kovelant figured his number was blocked on Julia's phone. He thought of stopping at a pay phone to try from a different number, but such things were almost nonexistent.

He was about to call it a day when Carl Hogan rang.

"First," Kovelant said, answering, "before we get to business: How's your day going? How's life, the wife, the strife of parenting. You've got three kids now, right? Two more since our little ones used to play. Fill me in. It's been too long."

"This can't be Detective Kovelant. Can I please speak to Detective John Kovelant? Who is this impostor? I do have something for you, though. You don't have to ask. I'm a giver, not a taker. Wife *loves* that, by the way. Best advice I can offer. Always give. Never expect to take, unless she insists, then always take."

"Same old Carl."

"This is weird," Carl said. "You're not dying, are you? I'm not doing your autopsy, if that's what you're asking. Not sleeping, maybe? See, here I am, giving. We've known each other, what, going on... twenty-something years? Twenty-three, twenty-four?"

"Let's round up. But seriously. How are you doing?"

You need to connect more, Amanda said, still looking out for him. *You can't be so disconnected from society the way you are. People need people*, she'd insist, the way hurt people tended to hurt people.

And it was true. He and Amanda had always been close,

understood each other intimately, especially following the loss of their daughter. Lilikoi. Forever three.

"You there?" Kovelant said.

"Yeah, just trying to remember where we left off. Us, I mean." Sadness, or nostalgia, softened his voice. "I'm, well, I guess you could say I'm doing all right. Molly's turning twenty-three this May and still living at home, looking for work. Emily's twenty and enrolled in the junior college. Josh, well, he's twelve, or 'twelve and a half,' as he likes to say, and on his way to challenge us with the mean-teens. And my partner, you know, same ol' same ol.'"

It *had* been a while. He'd missed most of their lives while he let his own spiraled downward. Last he saw Molly in person, the girls had been playing tricycle tag in his driveway, and he'd always pictured her that way. Carl's middle child, he couldn't even picture her face though he'd been shown digital photos at some point. And the boy, had he even known there was a boy? *Twenty goddamn years.* He'd received invitations for birthdays, baptisms, graduations. When had they stopped coming? When had he stopped going?

"I'm sorry, Carl," he said after some time. "After Lili—" but he couldn't say it, not yet, and not over the phone, and so he cleared his throat instead and he knew Carl would understand because that's the kind of man he was and the kind of relationship they'd carried all these years. "We need to whiskey again soon. Just you and me. Like we used to."

"That'd be great. But you're okay, really?"

"Yeah, just disjointed."

Silence separated them, the good kind.

"I really do have something for you," Carl said. "Something small. Not sure if it helps, but it answers one of your earlier questions. God, how do I even say this..."

"Tell me she wasn't pregnant."

A pause.

"I can't do that, John."

"*Jesus.*"

"A fetus develops most of its bone structure between sixteen and forty weeks. Found the smallest of ribcages, partial skull... not fully formed, which means earlier than sixteen weeks, is what I'm saying. A melted doll you could fit in your hand, and that's what it—" and a long sigh— "and amniotic fluid did its best to protect the child like it's supposed to, and the mother's own body, but they can only do so much to—such intense heat, well—*Shit-I'm-sorry*, John," he said, like one word. "It's part of my job to look beyond emotions, see things so no one else ever has or ever wants to—You of all people don't need to hear any of this."

"No, I do. Tell it to me straight, my friend. Everything."

"You sure?"

"Part of my job is a mix of motive and emotions."

"Emotivation?"

Sue Montgomery. How did she fit into this puzzle? Her profile: a barista; a friend to many, or so said the pictures on her wall; angsty, according to her coworkers, and a bit strange, but so were many twenty-something-year-olds; no known connection to the Bissets or Freemonts; both parents dead from a house fire when she was only seven; little girl playing with the gas stove and burning doll hair or melting faces; then off to the system and home-hopping until of legal age; clean record, otherwise. Yet she was an odd-shaped piece that fit into this somewhere, and so he thought he'd have a look at her apartment again.

He pulled up and parked in front of a moving van, which had its flat silver tongue lolling out with movers rolling in dollies stacked with boxes.

The door to the building foyer was wedged open with folded cardboard, and he nearly ran into a young fellow unable to see past the shade of the floor lamp he carried. The movers eyed him suspiciously but didn't seem to mind him going into the apartment complex. Most of the two-bedroom had already been hauled away. Boxes unlabeled, because who cared what was in them if they weren't going to be unpacked in a new home?

Sue Montgomery had died 'intestate,' as it went on her report—without a will—and with no next of kin to claim her belongings, and so all she owned went to the state to be dealt with however the state dealt with orphans. Sold. Donated. Burned or destroyed by some other means. He thought of Sue's childhood home burning, and then her body burning in that fiery crash. Holding the black husk of a doll in his hand. Couldn't get the images out of his mind. Two women clutched, no, *fused*, around an unborn child.

Lili had at least made it to three, but was that any better?

Amanda thought so, but he'd always thought it'd be

easier to have lost her earlier, or to have never had a child in the first place because of the world they'd be bringing her into.

He made his way into the kitchen.

GOT SEX? in the Montgomery home spelled out with refrigerator magnets had been changed to HOT SEX. He'd made a note of the messages on his first visit. One of the movers having some fun, most likely. Kovelant made his way there and changed the HOT to NO. WHAT COLOR IS THE WIND? was still there as well, although he hadn't been so interested in riddles in this case on his last go 'round. He searched for the answer on his phone and smiled.

Clever.

The rest of the apartment sat as an empty shell once full of memories: ghost outlines of dust where picture frames used to hang; unpatched holes in the plaster; stains on the carpet, both wine and grime like blood-splatter; a few cracked tiles in the bathroom, the shower rod still there, curtain gone; white walls in desperate need of repainting in just about every room, and power outlets painted over at some point by bad, too-hurried painters; the smell of ammonia from the place once housing a cat for so many years.

"That one's mine," a woman said behind him, and he turned to her. She pointed at one of the boxes. "See the name there in Sharpie? This entire *room* is my stuff. Not a lot left, but nothing from this room should be going." She'd died her hair black over the weird pinkish color and somehow made it worse. He tried to focus on her, but Carl's words kept plaguing him.

(develops most of its bone structure between sixteen and forty weeks)

Kovelant offered a broken smile.

"Ah, sorry, you're the cop, right?"

"You moving out?" he asked.

"Already did, but still had a few things here. I saw the moving van out front when I was driving by for work. You figure out what happened to Suse?"

(the smallest of ribcages)

"Suse?"

"That's what I called her, back when we were friends. She hated that I called her that. I mean, it's sad she's gone, what happened to her, but she'd turned into a real bitch. You know?" She bit her bottom lip, not to keep herself from laughing, but crying, her eyes glossing. "I don't mean to sound insensitive, but she'd upset all her old friends. Not just me."

"You didn't mention this before."

"Didn't think to, but yeah, someone even came in one night to, I don't know, prank her or something. Messed with the fridge. Ransacked her room. We had to repaint one of the walls or the property owner would have a fit. And I can thank whoever it was for *this*," she said, motioning to her hair. "Thought my head was bleeding in the shower. It shook me up. We had a huge fight and I moved out without half my stuff."

(partial skull)

"The fridge magnets?" Kovelant said, mostly to himself.

"Yeah. Left some weird messages for Suse. Even bit an apple and put it back. Who the hell does that?"

"Mind if I take them, see if I can find out who's responsible?"

"I don't care. About the magnets, I mean. They were here before us."

She followed him into the empty kitchen, and he took a pre-folded-together-and-taped box and knelt in front of the fridge. He started with NO SEX, which had once been HOT SEX, which had once been GOT SEX?—which he reasoned was the reverse order of how intimacy played out most times in life—and carefully slid them into the box with the back of his pen, not touching their surfaces, not letting them roll around. They'd have partial prints.

"Was she promiscuous?"

He opened the fridge, but it had been emptied out and cleaned. No apple.

"Suse, like with multiple people? As far as I could tell, she was *a*sexual," she said, really putting an emphasis on the 'a,' as if disappointed in that fact.

"And what night was this break-in?" Kovelant jotted down the date she provided, then pulled pictures of both Chloe Bisset and Kristoph Freemont from his pocket, but she shook her head no when he asked if she'd ever seen them or recognized the names.

"No."

"If I have any further questions," he said, "how can I reach you?"

The prints came back belonging to Kristoph Freemont, as he imagined they would. He had a misdemeanor on his record, nothing major—smoking pot in California before it was legal. *Still would be*, he figured, since he'd been caught smoking a joint outside a restaurant and had a decent-sized bag of buds in a Ziplock on his possession, and because consumption was not allowed in public spaces. The mugshot in the system was your typical sometimes-stoner: frazzled hair, wide but vacant eyes; could almost smell the stank on him through the screen.

The other partials weren't in the database but could have belonged to either of the women. No signs of the French woman in Sue Montogmery's apartment, but she'd been in there. One of those feelings he had in his gut. Chloe and Kristoph, partners in crime. Breaking and entering, at least. A 10-62. Why would they toss the apartment? To mess with the barista? Give her and her roommate a good scare? Typical motives were jealousy, revenge, money, drugs.

None of those felt right.

10
Results: Outcome / Conclusion

Chloe didn't quit her job that day. The impulse didn't strike. She managed, however, to tell the IT punk—who sighed like she was an idiot and an inconvenience when he came to unfreeze her computer—that he could stuff the attitude.

"What would you be doing with your shitty little life if it weren't for our glitchy system?" she'd asked him. "Your looks and your personality won't get you anywhere. Enough with the superiority and just fiddle those buttons so I can get back to work and you can go sit in your cave and play with yourself 'til the next call."

The words had come out automatically.

When he slouched off, red-eared and hands in his pockets, Chloe's colleagues on both sides gave silent golf-claps. But she didn't feel good about it. None of her actions, her impulses, stirred that same fever of excitement as that first day, and that first night.

"Check this guy out." Jules pointed his hotdog at the evening news. Onscreen, the anchor bit his knuckles in an attempt not to laugh, then cleared his throat.

Maxie had chosen dinner for the third time that week.

"You're going to start looking like a wiener if you're not careful," Chloe had warned and prodded her daughter's belly while she giggled. She imagined the child—not 'her daughter,' but just a child—taking far-too-large a bite, swallowing wrong, her face turning red, then blue, then ultimately pale. Then still. Silent. A short slice of chaos before an eventual, longer peace.

She and Jules sat on the ends of the couch with Maxie between them. Their daughter ate and stared at the screen. It never mattered what was on, if it was on Maxie sat transfixed. When exactly had this become the routine?

"Thought we were watching a movie. Is this live?"

"Happened a few hours ago," he said.

When did I first notice his voice was annoying?

Television had become a means to not talk, to not have to listen. They'd ask the same pointless questions about their day, a peck on the cheek, a reflexive 'love you'—and then they'd go right to the couch, their daughter there already, eyes unblinking.

"Maxie. What have I told you? Close your mouth." She'd gotten her eating habits from her father. Same open-mouthed *shlick-shlock* of food.

Chloe pressed on her stomach, a hot coal churning inside.

Too much crappy food taking its toll. Even their cooking had become lazy, a race to feed the kid, to feed the husband, using the microwave instead of the stove, boxes and bags instead of produce, fast food chosen over home-cooked. She'd have to eat salads for lunch, or she'd need new work clothes soon.

A wobbly recording of a construction site took up half the screen as a series of 'Oh my god!'s and 'What's he think he's doing?' narrated instead and pulled her attention.

Chloe put down her food. She recognized the locale. Downtown Sacramento, around mid-town. Her stomach churned with renewed dread as two things hit her: the feeling that this moment had already happened, and that she was experiencing it a second time knowing the outcome, yet this scene was novel and unfamiliar. On the other half of the screen the news anchor took over the narration.

"Spidey-man," Maxie said around a mouthful of mashed pink meat product and ketchup. She clapped her hands and leaned closer.

"This is not easy to see, so viewer discretion is advised. A man wearing a Spider-Man costume climbed the construction crane on—"

Shit.

"—and there he is now, crawling out onto the boom... And no, they are not filming yet another sequel or reboot in our city."

A buzzing in Chloe's ears.

"Maybe we should turn the channel," Jules said and slid his hand between the sofa cushions, feeling for the remote.

Chloe sat like her daughter: captivated, unblinking.

Ill-suited Spider-Man climbed out farther, halfway across the boom now, directly over the street a hundred or so feet up. He tugged at the red and blue unitard.

The black of deepest space, Chloe thought of what he uncovered. *Red and blue turning to nothing. Absence. The Void.*

The cell phone footage zoomed in, fuzzy, then not, though the person holding it shook increasingly as the crazy man tore at the thin fabric, revealing his hidden costume.

Jules paused in his search for the remote. "That's Venom. He's like the *anti*-Spider-Man. This has to be a publicity stunt."

The man peeled off the face covering to unmask a wide-open and fang-toothed mouth smiling ear to ear, long and lolling tongue hanging out. Charcoal black. A shadow against the blue sky. Stripped of the red and blue costume, he shook it in the air, mimicking defeat of the hero, and flung the fabric to the street.

He's fucking crazy. He—

"And then a flock of crows—attempted *murder*, you might say—appears to startle him, not liking that new costume, and I don't blame them, and—"

Jules put a hand in front of Maxie, the way he might if forced to brake hard. Chloe leaned back, awaiting impact.

The man lost his grip, slipped, and plummeted into the open air. And so did Chloe's stomach and she held it tighter. The black spider fell to certain death, the picture blurring as the camera followed him down. Gasps from the crowd of spectators.

Her own gasp caught in her throat.

How can they air this—

The camera lost track of him in dizzying disarray, then steadied and zoomed in on a rippling dark mass suspended halfway to the ground at the base of the crane.

"He [beep]ing jumped," the woman recording said.

"He's fucking crazy," Chloe said, which got her a look from Jules.

"Fucking crazy," Maxi repeated and clapped ketchup-red hands.

"Chloe."

"Not to worry, folks," the news anchor said, taking over. "Old Spidey landed in the safety net used to keep debris and equipment from falling onto traffic."

"Sorry," Chloe said, out of habit. "Maxie, don't say that, 'kay?"

The footage switched to a proper news camera. Firefighters struggled to untangle the resisting man from the net, cuffed him, pulled off his second mask, and placed him in the back of a police cruiser. Even with his face blurred, Chloe knew him. Pressed her hand to her mouth.

The news anchor continued. "Turns out our friendly-turned-unfriendly neighborhood webslinger is a person of interest in a police investigation and has been taken in for questioning and psychiatric evaluation."

"City ordinance to the rescue," Jules said and slumped back into the couch, lowering his arm from his daughter— *his* daughter—and pulled the child close to wipe her hands.

The child; that's what she is to me. The child.

Chloe rose from the couch and hurried to the bathroom,

threw up into the toilet as quietly as she could with the running faucet as background noise. She rinsed her mouth, then fought the urge to speak her truths to the toilet once again, that awful, echoing sound against porcelain.

This is what he told me to watch for. What did he do?

When she got back to the living room, her phone buzzed on the coffee table, and she picked it up, her fingers going cold and shaky when she read the message.

You're it.

11

Je dis ça, je dis

I'm just sayin', John, it doesn't make any damn sense," Carl said over drinks, "but I have this weird feeling about what you'll find if you request the spider-freak's personal effects. Kristoph on his driver's license, and a ring inscribed with the French woman's name."

Free. Together. Forever, Chloe,

"Somehow I've always known, like I do now," Kovelant said into his glass of bourbon, "and I'm sure I'll know when time rolls over again." He had a sip left, but thought he'd let the ice melt to stretch it. "A recursive nightmare of past / present / future."

"That explains why your drink cost so damn much," Carl said. "This bottom-shelf swill never gets me thinking philosophically, only stupidly."

Kovelant thought of time constantly turning and repeating upon itself, a loop with ghost memories or recollections—*if that's what they are*—leaking out now and again through the cracks to gum up the cogs responsible for turning Time's wheel. He swirled his glass, lifted it to find a water ring on the bar—*rings, everything starts and ends with rings*—circled it with his finger, like an ensō symbol, lost in a meditative trance.

Free. Together. Forever, Kristoph,

Structure fire. He'd been called to a few post-fires, if deaths were involved, or crime, but there were no deaths involved with this one. Well, not directly. *Arson*, no doubt. Teams were still onsite combing the ashen debris for propane and water tanks, or anything else that might explode, and clearing paint cans and searching for other hazmat materials, which meant he had to wait longer than he'd wanted to before entering, despite the badge.

The place smelled and tasted like campfire.

A week later, according to dispatch notes, and the building still smoked in places. He wouldn't have even gone to check it out if not for the date it was started, and if the fire deputy chief hadn't replied when he called with "You gotta come see this."

Brick survived intense heat—how it was made, like ceramic and porcelain, also typically left behind in the rubble—and so the general structure of the building held up through the blaze, except for one windowed wall that had crumbled at some point and fallen inward.

Kovelant knew the place well, had driven by it plenty. Most of the windows had been blown out by rock-throwers over the years, ignoring the 'no trespassing' signs and 'smile, you're on camera' warnings, although no electricity ran to the place to surveille anything.

Besides the black running up the exterior of the smoldering ruins, the first thing he noticed were the windows, or lack thereof; the ones not boarded up had shattered or melted, hard to tell which.

"Every single window is gone now," he said to himself. "Every damn one."

A building with many hollow, punched-out eyes.

That's a whole lotta free coffees.

He'd caught a few kids tossing rocks here once, tempted by that glorious shatter of glass, but he'd let them go with a warning. Kids. After they'd biked off, scared, promising to never do such a thing ever again, *we promise, sir,* he'd been tempted himself to throw a stone. He'd always wanted to knock out a window when he was their age.

Now, outside the ruined building, he waited impatiently, thinking of childhood and the childhood his daughter never had and what that did to him and Amanda over the years— how they'd both grown apart and together—and thinking of what it must be like to hold a blackened fetus in the cup of your hand. A small percentage of people could do that without absolutely losing their shit. The courage it must take to move past the emotion and embrace the science, the way Carl had daily for as long as he'd known him... but someone had to do it, and he respected his friend for that great sacrifice.

Lost in thought, he startled as someone knocked a knuckle on his driver's side window. A man in full hazmat with a ventilating facemask pulled free gave him a thumbs-up, then pointed to the destruction. He opened the door, immediately greeted by the fire deputy chief.

"Heard you were coming. Thought I'd say hi."

"Hey, Bill."

Bill's hands were gloved, and filthy, so both men did the nod thing, and sometimes that was enough of a greeting.

"You're here for the graffiti."

"I am," Kovelant said.

"You'll need to put these on."

Familiar with the process, he put the white booties on over his feet, slipped on a pair of latex-free rubber gloves, then the N-95 facemask. A refuse bin had already been placed by the entrance—wooden doors long gone, now just an opening—where he could toss it all after, lest he bring future cancers home with him.

"All right," Kovelant said. "Show me."

A cigarette called for him, badly, or another drink. A strong one.

The deputy chief led him through the building, what was left of it, every step placed carefully, although a path had been cleared. The once red-brick walls were now mostly gray, blackest at the bottom, and the roof completely gone and exposing the night sky. Halogen lamps illuminated the interior brighter than daylight.

"The fire started there," the deputy chief said, pointing up to a room that no longer existed. They stood in the basement, necks craned. The first and second story flooring entirely gone. A finger directed his line of sight to a mound of plastic on the other side of the basement, with what resembled bent limbs poking out of it—a monster from any childhood nightmare casting its ugly mammoth shadow against the wall from the halogens. He couldn't help but be haunted by the "Arachnid" poem, and the two merged bodies that'd opened this case:

> *—bodies melded,*
> *skulls fused,*
> *torsos conjoined,*
> *metacarpals curled*
> *round one another*
> *into amalgamated fists—*

"Whoever did this used an accelerant to start that pile of desks and chairs aflame, then they fell through the floor at some point, so most of the damage is on this floor. Gasoline," he said pointing to what must have once been a gas can, now a twist of metal tagged as evidence. "Building held up, all things considered. But your words are up there near where it all started."

The heat of the ground fed up through his boots.

Adults wanting to fulfill childhood temptations. To be kids again, unconcerned about their futures, no fucks left to give.

"The call of the void," Kovelant said. "*L'appel du vide.*"

"What was that?"

"Nothing."

"Careful on the climb. I've got this." Bill stepped under the extension ladder that leaned against the wall and grasped the rails.

The ladder had been used over the years, survived many fires, but looked sturdy enough and rose twenty feet or so to what the deputy chief wanted to show him. Could have sent him pictures, but the dates matched, and "You gotta see this," he'd said, and Kovelant couldn't pass up that temptation. And so, he went up, hand-over-hand, through an absent floor that used to be a floor, and five rungs from the top he craned his neck to the east-facing wall and then the west, as instructed.

In a room that was no longer a room, spray-painted and fused to the plastered walls by fire: I WANT TO KILL MY WIFE on one side, and I DON'T WANT TO BE A MOTHER on the other. The messages coated by soot, and some letters gone, but decipherable.

Kristoph Freemont, Chloe Bisset.

One message his, the other hers.

Why attempt to burn down an old building... to hide what they'd emblazoned on the walls, their deepest, darkest secrets, their confessions?

One wanted to kill his wife. Had he fulfilled that wish by pushing her off the Discovery Park bridge? And the other no longer wanted to be a mother, leaving Maxie motherless. These two had conspired. United in a desire for change, or a return to a previous state...

After taking pictures and starting back down, he thought of Amanda. He'd been tempted on more than one occasion to begin a new life, but he hadn't been able to. Everything paused when Lili died, and he didn't know how to start again. He stopped for a breath midway and twirled his wedding band, loved how he couldn't slide it off, how it choked. He wiped his eyes as he rejoined Bill, blamed it on the smoke.

"You're right," Kovelant said. "I needed to see that," and he threw all the protective gear in the refuse bin on his way out.

The French had a term for 'the call of the void,' but did they have a phrase for eventually answering it? Then that damn poem again, something he couldn't shake:

> *Perhaps he was trying to save her;*
> *or maybe the other way around;*
> *could be he died inside her,*
> *coming with the fire.*

This is so messed up, this puzzle, the picture hideous.

"The living hell is that?" he said, returning to his vehicle.

A gargoyle sat on the hood, staring him down, eyes embers. A hairless cat. Ugliest fucking thing. The cat—if it could be called that—wasn't concerned by his approach, and jumped down to roll around on the curb, scratching its back or trying to rid itself of the godawful pink-and-bling collar. Looked malnourished, but hard to tell without any fur.

The fire do that? No.

"Kitty-kitty," he said, the way everyone greeted cats. He didn't like cats, but this one intrigued him. "You lost?"

He bent down to read the collar: no contact, just a name.

"Gotta be kidding me."

The hideous thing gave off a raspy purr like a rattle of dying last breath, its collar threading two weathered wedding bands.

12

Reporting the Outcome

Getting Jules drunk was the easy part. She'd sent Maxie to her mother's so they could have a 'date night,' and bought a bottle of his favorite whiskey, not so cheap.

"Just like the old days." She raised her glass to clink with his.

Chloe pretended to drink, dumping hers into his when he turned away, or taking her glass with her to the kitchen and pouring it out. The challenge had been getting him to bed before he passed out but drunk enough that he could only grope her a little before snoring.

Love you too, honey.

Purse and car keys in hand, she watched her husband sleep. Part of her wanted to climb back in with him. Exhausted. So tired it was an effort most days to even move. She hadn't been this tired since—

Jules moaned and stirred, hand reaching across the bed to where she should be. His wedding ring had to go. She had taken off the ring he'd wed her with, releasing him, but *his* ring still tethered her. A symbol, sure, but their marriage had been the first link in the chain that bound her. Constricting. Smothering.

Chloe tugged, but the ring stuck on his knuckle. Jules clenched his hand, then stilled. She stroked his wrist until he relaxed, his fist unfurling one finger at a time, smile on his face. With a squirt of the lube she kept in her nightstand, she finally twisted the ring free, then fished the band Kristoph had given her out of her purse: *séparé*. The new ring slipped on a little too easily.

Jules would eventually notice the new band. How could he not?

Separated, or *apart*.

A problem for a different day.

The barista hadn't been home, so she'd slid a note under the door suggesting they meet the following night. No way she could repeat the 'whiskey until blackout' tactic, so she drove around after work until the appointed hour. And now Chloe sat at The Stagger Inn, twirling her finger in her glass of tonic-sans-vodka, the ice cubes pinging against the sides.

'Nikki' was late. No surprise there. The surprise was that the woman had agreed to talk to her. Hours after she'd left her note, a text popped up on her phone with a location and time. She wrote it down on a Post-It in case her cellphone died; with everything else going on in her mind, she'd forgotten to charge it and the phone was down to a single-digit percent.

The sense of dread—the one that kept her awake at night, sweating and restless for action—surged each time the door to the bar swung open. She supposed it was a blessing that most patrons staggered out rather than in, but that thought didn't lighten her mood. The clenched fist of anxiety in her gut tightened as the clock ticked, to the point where she felt she'd purge whatever was in her. A terror gnawing its way to the surface.

From her seat at the bar, Chloe checked out the patrons at the tables behind her, reflected in a smoked-glass mirror that hung behind a meagre assortment of bottles. Between the Jim Beam and the Jack Daniels a pair of lumpy middle-aged men in work shirts slouched, grasping half-empty pint glasses. They spoke occasionally, glanced at the door when it opened, rubbed their faces with thick-fingered hands. Chloe decided they were long-haul truckers, their mutual acquaintance, the road, the only thing they had in common.

She wondered what truth each of them held secreted away in their deepest, darkest thoughts. Booze-numb, eyes dry and burning from staring at endless miles of highway, did they climb in the back of their cabs and *wish wish wish* for something terrifying? Something wonderous? The leather-skinned woman in the red PVC miniskirt at the stool closest the door—her truth couldn't be more obvious. A simple, yet impossible need to be young and desired. The second guy to approach her and offer a drink stank of cheap whiskey, aftershave, and sweat. He, and the rest of the drinkers, wanted something more primal. They slouched in this worn-down room and drank themselves closer to it, or drank to forget the truths Chloe chose for them:

My parents never loved me.

Greed consumes me, and yet I hunger for more.

I only feel pleasure when I hurt someone.

I will never be happy.

I am to blame for everyone leaving me.

Yet none of those were as horrifying as her own truth.

She took another sip of tonic, too sweet without the bite of vodka.

Just one shot to take the edge off.

Jules wouldn't notice her breath, considering the shape he was in today. She thought back to putting a hole in the wall, which seemed so long ago, then looked at her hand, the new ring gleaming innocently. Did she feel different? Had there been a sense of release when she'd lifted the portrait and dropped in Jules's wedding band, heard it ping against the golf club, or was that the relief of getting away with something, again?

In the mirror, the barista's scowling face appeared between rainbow bottles.

"Should have known the note was from you." Nikki snorted and shook her head. "People like you always cause drama, mess things up. Thanks for the crap you pulled in my apartment. My roommate moved out, left without settling up on rent."

"Sorry," Chloe said, though she really wasn't. "I just don't understand what's going on. Why am I doing the things I'm doing?"

Nikki took off her over-sized army jacket and draped it atop the stool, signaled the bartender, then sat. "You're buying, right?" she said, and then to the bartender, "I'll have a cognac. Double."

"Another virgin vodka tonic for you?" the bartender wiped her hands on the towel draped over her shoulder.

"I'm good."

"What kind of backwash drink is that?" Nikki said, mostly to herself.

Chloe's phone buzzed, but she ignored it. Already today she'd received eleven messages. How did Kris even have access to a phone? He was supposed to be undergoing treatment in the psych ward, according to the papers. All his texts were similar:

You know what you must do.
You must finish it.
Remember your truth.
Finish it.
Be free.

The barista's drink arrived, and she held the glass up to her nose, sniffed, then threw it back and signaled for another. "So, you guys go on a rampage, lighting fires, breaking into peoples' homes, doing whatever you want, and you are surprised it went to shit?"

"I can't stop. I don't know how. And I'm scared of what I might... how it's going to end." Chloe's voice cracked, and she took a sip of tonic, wishing again it had alcohol, but terrified what a few drinks might invite her—*allow* her—to do. "I think he's done something terrible, and I think I might, too.

Not because I want to, but because I *must*. He says we made a deal—with each other, with something else—I don't know. How do I end it without keeping up my end?"

"Most deals, if you don't keep up your end, it'll only be worse." Nikki shrugged. "Least that's what I learned in my classic lit course. Then you have the trickster character—he always tries for the workaround. That goes badly for him most times, too."

Tears stung Chloe's eyes. "So, there's nothing you can do?"

"Me? What the fuck would *I* be able to do? I'm not turning you in to the cops if that's what you're wondering. This is all on you." Nikki stood and swung her coat around her shoulders. "If you get a chance, let me know how things turn out. I do like a good ending."

The barista's reflection disappeared beyond the rainbow and out the door as Chloe twirled what was left of the ice with her straw. She didn't want to go home. Maxie was there. And so were the thoughts. At any moment, impulse could turn to action.

The more she pushed the thoughts back, the more often they came, and the closer they moved from notion to the unthinkable. And yet she thought them:

How long do you have to hold a pillow over a child's face before they stop struggling to breathe? Is it common for children to drown in the tub? Is it painful? What if a child mistook rat poison for sugar, or pain meds for jellybeans? If a child falls out a window, would she bounce when she hit the ground, or split open like a jug of milk? Would she lose consciousness before impact? Is the Pacific Ocean cold enough to induce hypothermia? One of the more pleasant ways to die, isn't it? A distracted driver wouldn't even notice a child pushed out onto the street at just the right moment. Does a child cry out for her mother as she dies, even if her mother is the bringer of death?

Her throat swelled with a scream she couldn't release, her breath caught behind it. The images came, relentless. Would the impulse come next?

Nikki had to know something. She was the one who set all this in motion, wasn't she? This was not a natural course of events. Chloe wouldn't act the way she did, think these things, if she weren't under some form of influence. Riddles were tricky things. There had to be a different ending. The second snifter of cognac, untouched on its coaster, gleamed amber-gold.

Chloe's phone buzzed, and then again. She thought of dropping her phone in the tonic, wondered what kind of noise the phone would make drowning. What she wouldn't give to be untethered...

There were two messages from Jules.

She tapped her glass with the phone, nearly gave into the urge.

The first message from him read: *You can't still be at work? Call me*; and the one prior: *M missed you reading her bedtime story. Goodnight Moon AGAIN. Home soon? XX*. And before that, three identical messages from Kris:

Finish it.

Finish it.

Finish it.

Chloe grabbed Nikki's cognac and dumped it in with her

watered-down tonic. She sipped, then took a proper swallow. It burned and she wanted more, though her stomach took a moment to settle. But she still didn't know what her next move should be.

She pulled out her credit card and slid it across the counter for the bartender. Another clue dropped if Jules ever checked; another sign they were in trouble—*she* was in trouble. But he would never look, never see how she'd stepped off that worn path of theirs, leading from marriage to the final contractual parting.

She stood to leave, bent to grab her purse from the floor, and spotted a wallet under Nikki's stool—one of those old-fashioned billfold / coin purse combos—alligator skin with a glittery clasp. Cool and oily. Chloe held it below bar-level and pried apart its various cavities, looking for ID. A silver earring in the shape of an ankh slid out, missing its backing, as well as coins from countries she couldn't imagine the barista visiting: Japan, Mexico, Egypt, Italy, and scraps of paper with half-written riddles in faded letters.

She squinted, only able to decipher one of them.

What is it, that given one, you'll have either two, or none?

"I hate these things."

The bartender slid her card and receipt across the counter.

Chloe put the wallet in her purse, walked out to her car, and ignored the new messages and the pop-up that warned her phone was about to expire. She searched for the answer to the riddle.

A choice.

What choice did she have?

She pictured Kristoph in a padded cell babbling like a cartoon villain about chains and freedom. The wedding ring he had given her, slightly bigger than her original, had bruised the fingers on both sides, its shape unfamiliar, cumbersome. A new link in a new chain. A new path, but not worn by obligation; this path led into a looming darkness that concealed the terrain, the terminus. Did it branch somewhere in those shadows?

Were there such things as choices?

The wallet slid out of her purse onto the passenger seat as images flashed in Chloe's mind: red splatter on the apartment wall, that skin-and-bones cat with rings dangling from its bejeweled collar, painted truths dripping down a crumbling wall, a black figure plummeting into the void, flames consuming everything...

Chloe started the car.

When the trickster tried to change things, it went badly for him.

Most times.

Was that a hint? Was there another choice?

She pulled onto the highway—going too fast, cognac and tonic churning in her stomach, pistons pumping under the hood, blood pumping through her chest—and pictured her daughter, flushed pink and damp with sleep-sweat in a bundle of quilts, safe for the moment.

A lone car sped toward her.

The barista must have noticed her missing wallet. Chloe accelerated, spotted the pink plastic unicorn on the hood, horn poised like a jousting lance.

She sped toward the car.
Weaved.
Straightened.
They locked eyes.
How it en—

13
Le Vertige de la Possibilité

K ovelant sat across from Kristoph Freemont in the interview room of the psych ward—much like the interrogation rooms at the station. Bare walls. Empty. Nothing for the patient to use to bring harm to himself or to others. Too-bright florescent lighting. A sense of sterility. The patient restrained, but only enough to keep him at the other side. Unshaven. Pale. Two scratches marked the side of his neck. A bruise on his cheek, others hidden by the hospital-issued sweatsuit.

The cost of resisting arrest.

He put his hands on the table, and the man across from him did the same, mockingly. He splayed his fingers so Kovelant got a good look at his wedding band, and he couldn't *not* look at it. Plain, shiny, new. Not something he should have on his possession at the facility.

"You're here about Chloe," Freemont said, and then, like a sigh, "ah, *mon amour.*"

"What makes you say that?"

"If you were here about the other thing, I'm sure there'd be two of you. Good cop, bad cop, am I right? And a lawyer, state-appointed." The patient leaned forward, eyes wild. A real 51-50, this Kristoph fellow. "How is Chloe? Did she finish it?"

"What other thing?" he said, purposefully not answering the first question.

"Guess not, but did she?"

The ring was the same style as the one they'd found on Chloe Bisset's body in the wreckage, no doubt. Kovelant imagined this man prying it off and swallowing it like a pill, trying to free himself of this place and what he had coming to him, unable to choke and die because of the hole in the center, a horrible gagging, the throat unable to close over it. Like marriage: choking, but not always.

No point in drawing this out.

"You kill your wife?" he asked.

"Didn't you ever want to? Bet you have."

Not a grieving man.

"Never."

"No?"

Kovelant shook his head, thought about it. Once, long before Lili, he and Amanda had gone to the Grand Canyon. Not the one in Arizona, but the smaller one in Yellowstone up in north-west Wyoming, in the wedge tucked between Idaho and Montana. They'd hiked both the Upper and Lower Falls there. Truly breathtaking, as the drop in elevation stole air from his lungs when he leaned over the ridge, over the fall of water. Amanda jokingly nudged him. Heart pumping life through him, at that moment he'd smiled, thought of answering that call.

L'appel du vide.

"No," he finally said.

But there was that urge to nudge her back, that image of her losing balance and tipping / falling over the side, head-over-handlebars, her eyes as wild as this man's... sure, he couldn't deny there was a reason the French had come up with the phrase for this primal urge.

Freemont tapped his fingers on the table, a junky awaiting a fix—*Did she finish it?*—his ring *tap tapping* a beat, the handcuffs jingle-jangling. Kovelant wondered if this man smoked, part of his anxiety. Chloe Bisset and the spider corpse suddenly there in his mind—and, of course, he wanted a cigarette himself right about now.

The question had gone unanswered, about killing his wife, but the coal in his gut told him Kristoph Freemont had done it. He had pushed his wife over, had watched Julia Freemont fall and then land on that rock, head-first. A flash of red. He'd seen her twitching twenty feet or so below, still alive. Kovelant imagined him rushing to her, pulling her half out of the water, not to save her, but to make sure her head stayed beneath the surface to drown. And in doing so he'd smiled, having fulfilled that urge, and with that same hint of curved-lip Kovelant so desperately wanted to slap off this man's face.

And he'd then taken her ring, but why?

"What did you do with your wife's ring?"

"So, you *are* here with more than one agenda. My box is square / yet I am round / inside every tree / a bell's sound."

141

He held up the ring, said, "Get it? I bet she finished it. I bet Chloe finished it, which is why you're here."

"You like riddles, Kristoph?"

"What shines at birth and dulls with age, starts where it ends and itself never ends? What do fiancés, fiancées, and cell phones have in common? What is the same at its beginning and the same at its end but has no middle? Love ends with me, yet I'm made endlessly..."

"Listen, Freemont—"

"... and when dropped, I say my name."

Goddamn looney.

"What did you do with your wife's—"

"What holds two in love together but touches only one?"

Ring, ring, ring.

His cell phone vibrated in his pocket, buzzing along with this man's endless riddles about rings. No, he wouldn't get much out of him.

"I've got my own riddle for you," Kovelant said, "so pay attention closely." This hooked him, and so both leaned back in their seats. He watched the eyes; often the tell.

Kristoph Freemont practically salivated with anticipation.

"What color is the wind?" Kovelant said.

His eyes didn't say shit, but there was that smile, the mouth telling in more ways than with words. The man in front of him registered in that moment a multitude of information: that he had been in Sue Montgomery's apartment, had seen the riddle left on the fridge, had made some links with the clues, maybe not all of them—*or why else would I be here?*— and had found fingerprints there, matching, so careless.

Freemont sighed, which was also the answer, then said, "Kinda funny, those fridge magnets. I remember having those as a kid. Smelled like Play-Doh 'cause no one ever washed them, ever. Used to spell out things my mother didn't want me spelling out. Four-letter words, mostly: 'love' and 'hope' and 'head' and 'blow.' A shopping list, of sorts, or the opposite, since she either needed or gave those things— quite often to pay the bills and all, to raise a child. You were thinking other words, weren't you?"

"Your ring has an inscription"—another twitch-smile, another glimmer—"and when you take it off and hand it to me, I'll tag it as evidence... where was I?"

"The inscription," Freemont said, slipping off the ring. He inspected the band himself, held it out then pulled it back all cat-and-mouse. "You got a warrant?"

"I don't need a warrant for the ring. You're not supposed to have it here.

Kovelant pulled a pair of rubber gloves out of his pocket, snapped them into place as though intimidating a suspect with a cavity search, then held out his hand.

"You're a detective, smart guy," Freemont said. "You already know the inscription." He cleared his throat, tested a few notes with varied hums, then sang out, "Spider-*man*, Spider-*man*, does whatever..." holding the note for a good three seconds, "... a *spi*der can." His voice broke trying to hit too high a note toward the end. "I was gonna dive, graceful as a swan, off the end of that boom. Damn birds made me lose my footing in the wrong spot. You saw the news, right?"

"Why? I mean, why everything," Kovelant said, trying to

make sense of madness. "Not just the crane, although I have to admit that yeah, you got a laugh out of me, but burning down an old building due for demolition anyway, what you did to your wife, and Chloe Bissett."

"*Mon amour*," he said, rotating the band around his finger.

"The ring," Kovelant said, not too kindly.

"Right." The chain attaching the handcuffs to the table let him reach halfway across, and he dropped the ring, which *spun, spun, spun*, finally settled. Both watched, mesmerized.

Free. Together. Kovelant slid the ring closer, rotated it 180° to read what Freemont was reading from his perspective. *Forever, Chloe.*

"You killed your wife," Kovelant said. "She reached out to you as she fell, one last time. Remember that? I hope the look on her face flashes forever in your mind. She scratched your neck, two fingers." He pointed two fingers at the parallel scabs on the patient / prisoner. "Forensics found skin under her nails, just this morning, left pinky and ring finger, go figure. After I leave, the inside of your cheek's going to be swabbed. They'll find a DNA match."

Kristoph shrugged. He wasn't worried he was caught. That was part of the rush, part of the call, if that's what it could be called, this impulse that drove him.

"So, she did it," Freemont said and smiled fully. "Chloe finished it."

"You killed her, too. I just need to figure out how."

"She got what she wanted," Kristoph said. "You just can't accept it."

Kovelant parked at Sue Montgomery's place, not intending to go inside again, but to think. A place linked to a case sometimes got the cogs in his mind turning. He leaned the seat back and stared up at her apartment. Empty now, but not, he figured, now filled with ghost memories. The rearview reflected a marigold swallowed by cityscape.

Sank eight-plus minutes ago, our sun, but the light's still there.

Looking into the future requires looking into the past; his father had told him that looking up at the stars, even our own, was time travel. "Your past don't matter," he'd said, "only your future," but he was wrong because detective work required the past.

He imagined Chloe Bisset standing at Sue's window, peering down at the creep peering up at this woman who no longer existed. She'd open the window, wave. She'd light the cigarette Kovelant craved, a French brand on a long, slender cigarette holder, the end burning an orange hole in the night as she took a long drag.

The ember transformed into the blinking red light of a smoke alarm on the apartment ceiling.

"Fuck it," he said, and got out.

Sue, or 'Nikki' if she swapped her nametag, lived across from a convenience store, and the bell above the door signaled his entrance to the man behind the counter.

Neither spoke, both nodded.

"Pack of Marlboros," he said with a twinge of guilt, his old brand.

It would always be his brand.

Yes, he *needed* a cigarette.

Another nod from the clerk.

The pack begged for him, then beeped when scanned.

He thought of a polite 'never mind' but the clerk had already rung him up, and now he no longer *needed* a cigarette—just one, only one—but *wanted* to fulfill that urge. A regression to the time before. And he felt just as nervous buying this final pack as he did buying his first.

Déjà vu.

No reason to check his ID this time around—*not that anyone did back then*—because Kovelant looked far older than his years, weathered from the job or stress or mileage, his skin tough and textured as leather. The man behind the counter recognized that tired face.

He'd questioned the clerk about the girl who lived across the street. She sometimes came in for junk food, sometimes alcohol, the typical impulse purchase. When shown a picture of the French woman, he'd said that she'd recently come in, said *merci* when leaving.

"You need a lighter?"

Kovelant eyed the display, said, "just some matches."

He dug in his wallet and slid a ten across the counter and received not a lot of change in return. Last time he'd smoked, a ten bought a carton. The pack felt lighter too as he hefted it and slapped the end against his palm to get the tobacco all to one side. Something his father did.

Outside, Kovelant struggled with the plastic wrap, tapped the pack a few more times, then opened and slid out a cigarette. It fit between his lips like a missing piece.

"Every moment has purpose," his mother used to say.

He leaned against his car and wondered at this. The match flared. He stared up at the dead woman's apartment windows and smoked with the ghost of her. Tapped off ash. Inhaled smoke. Exhaled streams that clouded the chilly air. The faint ember of Chloe Bisset's manifested cigarette blinked on and off as regular as his own puffs. He thought of her and Kristoph Freemont rummaging through the apartment with 'Nikki' gone.

A thump on his hood startled him out of the moment.

The Void sat on the top of his car, mischievousness glistening and green in its eyes from the streetlamp. *Tapetum lucidum*: the term for the retinal reflection coming to him at once, something he'd learned long ago. The cat—whichever of its nine lives it currently lived—let out an awful sound, as though saying, "The fuck you doing here?"

The cat judged him silently.

"I know," he said. "Bad habit."

He dropped the cigarette in the gutter, grinding it with his shoe to complete the ritual. They were designed to decompose he'd read somewhere, but still he picked it up and tucked it in his pocket. An imprint of pucker stayed on his lips, dried them out.

He snapped a photo of the cat with his phone.

On his previous encounter, he'd been able to rub its hairless belly, but it scurried off before he could take what he wanted from it. The two rings still threaded the pink collar. He'd imagined what they'd think at the station if he put out an APB on a cat.

Kovelant said the typical "kitty-kitty" and held out his left hand as an offering. The Void came to him, buried its shriveled walnut-like head into his palm and stutter-purred. He linked the two rings with his own and looked up again to Sue Montgomery's window—'Nikki'—expecting her there this time instead of the French woman. "This was your cat," he said, and the realization, "*Shit*," because it was going to need a new home.

He gave the cat some love, let it walk around on the hood of his cruiser, making little pawprints. The cat didn't lose interest and run off this time, but stayed with him, and in that time, he was able to twirl the smallest ring to read à jamais inscribed within. He didn't know the French word, but knew it was Chloe Bisset's original ring, and that it completed the phrase when combined with her husband's ring: *séparé*. The other ring didn't have an inscription, so he assumed—knew—it once belonged to Kristoph Freemont.

More love, then he unlatched the pink-bling collar.

The cat sat, tilted its head, still purring.

à jamais *séparé*

"Don't worry, you'll get it back."

Kovelant removed the rings and slid them into his shirt pocket and was about to return the collar to its rightful owner when The Void called. The cat uttered a guttural yowl and spun around on the hood. Another sense of *l'appel du vide* hit him with its cry, an urge to give the rings back. But no, that wasn't right. He let out a long sigh and scratched the cat's neck to keep it there longer.

"Hold on," he said, "this might take a while," and it did.

The cat waited patiently.

His wedding band stuck at the knuckle. His finger had grown fat around it after so many years. A band of burden. He and Amanda had talked about renewing their vows, so long ago, and they should have. But that was in the past, and a part of them that never made it into their futures. Everything was stuck in the past. Lili, little Lilikoi, was stuck in the past. "Your past don't matter," his father had said, "only your future."

"Maybe he was right... *almost got it—*"

His ring cut into the flesh of his knuckle, the blasted finger about to dislocate if he pulled any harder, and the mix of sweat and blood finally freed and flung it into the air. Arcing, reflecting streetlight, his wedding band clinked the curb and then asphalt, rolling toward Sue Montgomery's apartment. The red light blinked through the window. She wasn't there. The ring came to an abrupt stop against the opposite curb, inches from a drain. Kovelant ran to it, adrenaline pumping through him. His finger throbbed.

Not too many cars out, so he J-walked.

He brought the ring back to the cat—still on the hood of his cruiser—and threaded it through the pink collar, then reclasped it, rubbed the cat's hideous head.

"I need to move on, right? The law of life is change."

The Void seemed satisfied and went on its way.

§

He decided to meet with Jules Bisset a third time. They'd spoken over the phone as the case ended, but it was time to fulfil a promise he'd made to the widower: that he'd get his wife's ring back to him.

Kovelant stood outside the door of the Bisset residence, hand poised to knock. He hesitated, listening for signs of what he should do. In his pocket were two evidence bags. One held the ring from the wreckage, the one he'd promised to return: *Free. Together. Forever, Kristoph*, worn by two women now dead. The bag other held the ring he'd found on the cat, the one that completed a message when matched with its pair: à jamais *séparé*. He had looked up the French phrase: *Finally, apart.*

"What holds two in love together but touches only one?" he said and knocked.

A ring.

His knuckle had swelled, still had the indention below it, the skin a lighter tone.

A ring sans ring, like a vodka sans tonic.

After meeting Jules, he needed a hard drink. A double, then another double, and a third. Carl was already at the bar, happy for the invite, and he wanted to try something other than the cheap stuff for once. They got snockered, laughed together, cried together. They caught up on life, for they had missed most of each other's over years of not-close-enough friendship.

"I gotta ask about you and Amanda?" he finally asked. "I noticed the, uh—well, I noticed what's no longer there, today, which is nothing, but *something* right? A little thing that means a bigger thing?"

Kovelant shot back the last of his current double. He'd lost count.

"I fucked it up, Carl. Lili needed her—Amanda—but *I* didn't. Especially after the accident. I tried, but over time it felt like I disappeared from our relationship." He wiped his mouth with his ringless hand. "I couldn't give her what she wanted, or make her feel wanted. It ended a few years after Lili died. I figured it was time to move on."

The pale band on his finger would fade in time. He still had time.

About the Authors

ERINN L. KEMPER'S fiction is published in anthologies such as *Behold! Oddities, Curiosities and Undefinable Wonders,* the *Chiral Mad* series, as well as *Tor.com, Cemetery Dance,* and *Black Static.* She lives by the Caribbean Sea where she runs on the beach with her dog, drinks too much coffee, and writes until happy hour. Her forthcoming novels include *The Patrons, Beneath Paradise,* and *Waves.*

MICHAEL BAILEY is a recipient of the Bram Stoker Award, Benjamin Franklin Award, and a Shirley Jackson Award nominee. He has published three composite novels, four fiction and poetry collections, and edits or co-edits anthologies regularly. He lives in Costa Rica where he is rebuilding his life after surviving one of the most catastrophic wildfires in California history, some of which you can read about in his collaborative poetry collection with Marge Simon called *Sifting the Ashes,* and in his forthcoming memoir *Seven Minutes.*

Made in the USA
Middletown, DE
28 April 2023

29627060R00092